Alabama
Chrome

Mish Cromer

LEAF BY LEAF

Published by Leaf by Leaf
an imprint of Cinnamon Press
Meirion House
Tanygrisiau
Blaenau Ffestiniog
Gwynedd, LL41 3SU
www.cinnamonpress.com

The right of Mish Cromer to be identified as author of this work
has been asserted by her in accordance with the Copyright, Designs
and Patent Act, 1988. Copyright © 2020 Mish Cromer
ISBN: 978-1-78864-913-1

Designed and typeset in Palatino by Cinnamon Press.

Cover design by Adam Craig © Adam Craig.

Cinnamon Press is represented in the UK by Inpress Ltd and in
Wales by the Books Council of Wales.

Mish Cromer is a writer and person-centred therapist from
London. Drawing on her cultural heritage of Greece and the USA,
she writes novels about the complexities of family, with a focus on
women's narratives and the meaning of home. She has a BA(Hons)
in English Literature from the University of North London and
worked as a Montessori teacher before training as a therapist. She
has three children and lives in London with her husband.

Acknowledgements:

My heartfelt thanks go to the following:
Jan Fortune, Rowan Fortune and Adam Craig, at Cinnamon Press, for taking a punt on Alabama Chrome, then putting in so much work, so steadily and smoothly, despite a pandemic and lockdown. Aki Schiltz and the team at The Literary Consultancy. Alex Peake-Tomkinson for your skilful, detailed feedback. Alison Chandler, writer and teacher extraordinaire. Shanti Fricker and Anat Hinkis, for reading, sharing, and cheering me on. The patient and generous friends who found time to read and comment with intelligence and heart: Tracy Harvey, Lindsay Masters, Jenny Olivier, Susan Olivier, Harriet Wheeler, Marianna Weiner. Francis Bainton, for your thoughtful comments and encouragement. Little Molly, my Thursday companion and wise one. What would I do without you and your mama, Melanie Michelson? To my beloved sisters and brother, Cristina Cromer, Alice Pack-Beresford, Tom Cromer, for the laughs we have and the love you give.
Tom Frederikse, long ago you built me a safe harbour and have kept the lanterns burning ever since. Your constant support and love mean everything to me. Molly, Casey and Ruby, you are my inspiration. Nothing comes close to the love and respect I have for the three of you. It's you who remind me that spring comes.

For Tracy Harvey and Jenny Olivier

There is no agony like bearing
an untold story inside you.

                                Zora Neale Hurston

Alabama Chrome

1

If I don't make a decision right now it's going to be done for me, but the last one I made was for shit, and I knew it about five minutes after I left the interstate; this is a lonely road and the snow is squalling up so bad, I swear it's becoming a blizzard.

I can't ignore the rough-shod noise of my engine no more and there's a burned-out smell that brings me out in a cold sweat. I'm nauseous. I want to spit up. Cold is creeping right into me and making me stupid. I got no sense of where I am; I could be a hundred feet from the nearest town or a hundred miles.

Engine spits, drops, kicks back. It spews black smoke then cuts out altogether. I steer the van smooth as I can and let it coast to a standstill at what may or may not be the side of the road; for all I know I'm on the edge of a precipice. Probably am; these backwood mountain roads usually are. If I'm lucky there'll be trees to break my fall if I go over, but that makes me laugh and I think, Shit, I might be going a little crazy in this cold, because if there's one thing I'm not, it's lucky; they'll have been cleared for timber for sure and over I'll go, and right there would be your poetic justice.

I reach in back and grab the bedding, wrap it around me and then just sit. I sit, and try to keep my fear in check, while the snow tries to get inside. I can feel wind from all directions, right there inside the van, and I can hear it, sounding like hellcats screaming and howling out there in the nowhere. Every now and again the wind gets ahead of itself and almost lifts the van off of its wheels; it don't for one single moment stop rocking and banging about in the wind.

The cold keeps growing and crawling over me. I have on every piece of clothing I own, but still my belly tightens and shudders, my jaw clenches so rigid it hurts and my body starts a short, hard, tight jerking on the inside that goes on and on; I can't make it stop. And now I'm thinking strange, stupid thoughts about not being discovered till spring when the snow melts and uncovers my sorry ass and wishing I could tell Mama I love her. Right now, I wish that more than anything else in all the world. I want her to know it. And that I'm sorry.

My mind slips, slides away somewhere on thoughts of sunshine and water; a face smiling. The light around me is dazzling white and I can't keep my eyes open no more. I shove my hands hard into the pockets of my coat, my shoulders bunched up around my neck so they ache, but I can't relax and can't stop my body from shuddering so hard I'm sure I'm about to bite through my tongue. I close my hand around the little box in my pocket and shut my eyes.

A dull thumping fills my head. Maybe it's outside me somewhere, I can't tell. Keeps on. Shut. Up. Please just let me, just let me sleep.

Muffled voices come from way off somewhere. I open half an eye, before the bright pierce of white light, a tilt of icy blue, makes me shut it tight again. I wonder if it's God calling me and think of laughing, but this time I can't get further than the thought. I can't seem to make anything work.

Face of an old man is pressed up against the window and I wonder if that's Him; A girl's face comes into view and I think, now angels, but they don't got fur lined hoods so far as I know and this makes me a little more determined to make out what she's saying. I think it'll be easier when I'm not so tired, so I turn away and try and ignore these clowns outside banging and thumping away, making out like I should follow the light.

Next thing I know, my fucking window's been broke and I try and holler at them to get away, that I have a weapon, but the words don't come and the girl, she's crawled through the back and she's unlocking the door and shoving at me and pulling and yelling things in my face and I give up. There's no fight left in me and, truth be told, it's been that way longer than I care to remember.

I'm in the cab of a high up truck, heat running, blanket wrapped around me, shivering so hard my teeth rattle and I'm sure I'm about to knock 'em right out. Angel in the fur hood is trying to get me to drink something steaming from a flask and talking up how lucky it is she took this route to work, otherwise who knows how long it would a been before somebody came across me. Old fellow posing as God is driving and tells me his name is Beau and that I'll be alright now.

'Lark,' he says to the girl and I, stupid as I am, feel a lift that she's a bird and not an angel; a creature like that is something I can believe in. 'What do you say we take him to my place and see what's what?'

'Is Belle about?' she asks, and the fellow tells her to use his cell phone and give her a call.

It ain't no time before I'm sitting in his home by a wood burner, spooning some kind of thick soup into my clumsy mouth and trying to make sense of what's going on. I can't seem to make my fingers work right and worry I'm going to spill the soup. I put the spoon down and try focusing on whatever might be out of the window; ain't much to see. The house stands in a clearing, that much I noticed when we pulled in. From here I can see the snowy yard, snow topped fencing, and a big ol' barn with doors wide enough to take a tractor. A little way down the trees begin again.

The girl, Lark, comes over from the kitchenette and stoops to pour my soup into a big coffee mug. 'Try it this way, you're still so frozen it's bound to be hard to hold anything right now.' She hands me the mug and I close my hands around it, try not to shudder and lose the lot. 'You got a name we can call you?' She smiles.

I think for a moment, trying to get in gear. 'You can call me Cassidy,' I tell her. I lean back and close my eyes.

They talk together, real quiet, but I'm too tired to pay any attention anyhow and feel myself drift, before I whap my eyes open, startled by the feel of the mug slipping from my hands. It's just her, though, the girl, taking it before I drop it, sweet look in her eyes. 'Okay?'

I nod.

When the old fellow, Beau, is good enough to offer me a bed for the night, I speak up.

'You don't have to do that. You don't even know me.'

He gives me a puzzled smile, gentle. 'I know you need a bed,' he says, and he looks right at me until I can't meet his eye no more.

'Thank you,' I say. 'I appreciate your kindness.' I'm overcome with shame that I might cry in front of these strangers.

The next day, me and Beau make a trip to the local mechanics. We drive up a single-track from his home, leaving the creek, and woods behind us. Cab of his truck is warm and quiet. He don't ask too many questions, just gives out a little here and there.

'Look up there to your right. See that cottonwood?'

It's a beauty, real tall, and I think how it might look in summertime.

'I ain't never seen one that big,' I say, and I see him crinkle at the edges of his eyes.

'We entered it for Champion Trees of Kentucky a while back,' he says. 'Got ourselves a special mention.'

I don't ask what that is, and it don't matter on account of he's pointing out Main Street and showing me where his lady, Belle, has her beauty parlour.

'That's it right there with the pink and green awning, next to what used to be our local newspaper. But that's gone now you young people get all your news online or from the TV.'

'That's too bad, I guess,' I say, thinking that's what he means.

'Well, I'm not averse to progress, and that's a fact, but it does seem a shame that every time something closes, more folks move away, aside from your old fool diehards like myself, of course.' He does a rumble deep in his chest I understand to be his laugh, but sobers pretty quick and says, 'But don't get Belle started on that. Her pet project is…' he breaks off to check his mirror and pull across to the other side of the road and eases in at the kerbside next to High Beam Auto Repairs and Diagnostics.

'Now, let's see if we can't get you back on the road and on your way.' I guess I'll never know what Belle's pet project is.

I get in front of him and hold open the heavy plastic curtain hanging over the open doorway and he goes in ahead of me. The floor is cement and oil, dirty rags and tools. Up on the wall, an old tube style TV is hanging out, tuned in to KYTV and turned up loud, trailing one of them reality shows Mama used to give the finger: Brooke Adler's *Random Acts of Kindness*. There's a music radio station on too and the sound of a blow torch working hard. Whole place smells good and familiar to me.

Somebody's legs are sticking out from under a tow truck, greasy blue overalls and work boots are all I can see of him.

'Is that you under there?' Beau asks, bending to look. 'Fellow here might have some work for you.'

Mechanic shoves a foot, comes rolling out on the dolly and sits up, reaching a hand out to Beau, who grabs it and pulls.

'Well who the hell else is it going to be, Beau? You think there's ever going to be enough work in this town for me to hire help?'

I get that feeling of surprise that makes me want to kick myself; Mama'd be shaking her head at me right about now. 'I raised you better'n that,' she'd tell me. 'Never assume, it makes an ass out of u and me.' I got so tired of that old joke I stopped hearing it, which tells you something maybe about how long it takes me to learn a thing. Or not.

Anyhow, the mechanic ain't a fella at all, but a woman about my age maybe, thirty some and real tall and rangy, backwoods to the core; she got that pale-eyed, cagey look but it disappears the minute she smiles, which she does just about every time something comes out of her mouth, just not at me.

'Hey,' she says, leaning back against the truck and wiping her hands down her pants legs. 'You must be the guy Lark pulled out of the snow. Lucky she came by.' She turns her look on Beau again. 'Did you ever see anything like it? Lark says her mama'n daddy remember an ice storm one spring to rival it, killed every last sprout they'd planted, but never saw a snowstorm like this in all their years farming.'

'I can't say I ever have,' Beau tells her. 'And damage to spring crops is going to be bad.' He turns and puts a hand on my shoulder, and I flinch before I can think and that old fellow, he just squeezes and lets go with a pat, like he's quieting a horse. 'Cassidy, Evangeline here is our local doctor of all things to do with engines, like her daddy before her, and if she can't get your van back on the road, it's not going to happen.'

'Lark says you'll need your van towed?'

I nod, but I'm unsure of what I need, and I'm concerned that towing is just the tip of this iceberg; I think again about the noise and smell and swallow hard.

Evangeline is looking at me, suspicious and I would say, unfriendly. 'Let's get something straight, right off the bat. I

14

do not run a good-will service here. Unlike everybody else in this damn town. I'm not towing no van for charity, you got it?'

'Now look here, Ev,' Beau starts in, 'least you can do is get that sucker off the side of the road. It's a hazard to all and as far as I can make out,' he turns to look at me then and says, 'it's your home, am I right?' I nod and look at the doorway. 'If we don't move it soon, someone else will and Cassidy here will lose anything he owns.'

'Well, I can't bring it here,' Evangeline tells him, grudging. 'I don't have the space. Unless you're good for the money,' she says at me.

Something sparks then, inside me, fires up for a second and I look right back at her. Hard ass, I think, but truth be told I kind of admire her straight talk.

'Do I look like a body who has any money?' I ask her then, and she raises an eyebrow at me. First time, right there, that her smile is at me.

'Levi's looking for help,' she says and I'm struck by a thought that leaves me feeling empty; I'm now a man with nothing better to do, no call on his time nor company; it don't make no difference to nobody if I put up in a broken down mountain town and take a job.

'Levi's always looking for help,' Beau cuts in.

'What kind of help?' I ask and the mechanic, she gets that look that tells me I ain't no better than I am, who the hell am I to be picky?

'Bar work. Does it matter? It pays.'

And I think, well, she's right. Does anything matter? I put my hand in my pocket and tap, tap, my finger on the little box.

Beau offers me a ride to Levi's, but I'm done being inside of things for now.

'I'll stretch my legs,' I tell him. 'Get a feel for the place.'

15

Evangeline snorts. 'Looking for the bright lights?' she asks and lowers herself onto the dolly again; she sure is salty.

Outside, Beau points the way we came, and tries to talk me out of walking.

'Forecast says clear,' he tells me. 'But it's real cold and about to get colder. You don't want to be doing yourself another bad turn in the cold now, do you?' But there's something in his manner, unhurried, kind, like he won't take it bad if I make up my own mind.

I set out on foot to get to know the place. It's an old habit I have from a child.

When Mama and me came again to a new place, I'd roam about getting a feel for it, barefoot if I could, until I could find my way about in the dark if I cared to.

The auto shop is lonely on its own, just outside town, and the walk is further than I imagined. I get to wondering if I didn't miss the turn in the road. There ain't no kerbside, which is usual in these parts, so I walk along the paved road, keeping my ears sharp for oncoming vehicles.

Beau weren't wrong; it is cold. And what began as a clear, pretty day, is fast clouding up and I'm starting to miss the winter sun that was. I pull the collar of my jacket closer around my neck.

A movement snags at the corner of my eye and right away lifts my spirit a little; I always did like to pace myself alongside a woodpecker. I like the way they fly; dipping and rising and getting ahead, then waiting. It's a friendly sort of game, trying to see if you can catch up while it waits at the next tree, or electricity pole. When I was a boy, I liked to think they was showing me the way and I let myself think that right now.

I keep walking, striding long to get my blood going. I can hear the crunch of my feet on grit, but the snow, still laying out over everything, seems to muffle most other sounds excepting for the one or two that are sharper to my ear than they might otherwise be; silence and birdsong, calling and answering each other, and just for a moment the world good and clean. If I could just stay right here, with nothing but the birds and the trees to contend with, and this cold, sharp air that numbs everything, I might be okay.

The woodpecker gives up on me and starts pulling at loose bark, getting at something good to eat. I stop to watch him for a moment before the cold slides up my legs and presses at the bones behind my ears.

About a half hour after I leave Beau, the road widens and the trees thin out, and I find myself coming out into the open, the tarmac road widening out and sloping away towards a long, low row of square, flat-fronted stores and buildings. There's a white striped painted crossroad, but only one of the crossings seems to take you anyplace. The other leads you straight into a big old pine-mulched bed of shrubs, weighed down with snow.

The square, brick, building on the corner, white paint peeling off of it everywhere you look, has a patchwork of bright painted murals telling you to LOVE where you LIVE *historic* **Horse Neck Creek** *don't drink and drive, y'all!* Aside from that, there's not a whole lot else to see.

I look about for the striped awning Beau showed me before and follow his directions to Levi's Bar and Grill.

It stands in a dirty old parking lot, set back from the kerbside, with overfilled dumpsters and oil spills and who knows what else staining the paving. The whole place looks tired-er than me and just as used to it.

There ain't no windows, and the metal door must be a security service put up after the bailiffs come in. I take a moment to wonder if Beau and Evangeline was messing with me; Levi's long dead and gone and nobody's home; nobody's looking for help. But fixed above the flat roof is a red, neon sign, fizzing a little every now and then and telling me this here is Levi's and there's an arrow swooping down towards the beat-up metal door to emphasise the point.

Now I wouldn't put it past that salty car mechanic to mess with a stranger for her own type of fun, but I can't think it of Beau, so I pull at the door and it opens easy enough into a storm lobby papered all over with flyers telling about hardwood for sale, a deal on a four by four with trailer, and an All U Can Eat Pit Barbecue long since passed.

Tacked up onto the glass in the saloon door is a piece of paper reading: *Last day to sign up for this month's grocery run is the 21ˢᵗ, that's THIS COMING THURSDAY folks! Sorry! NO exceptions! Thanks for helping us make this happen! Lark and Belle x.* Somebody has drawn a little smiley face and heart next to their names.

Inside tells a whole different story to the sorry tale outside in the parking lot. It's a big, dark, barroom, but lit nice, with green and red coloured glass shades. It's longer than it is wide with framed photos over the walls of folks having wholesome, country-style fun and there's a signed photo of what looks like it might be the inside of this very bar, with a band playing at one end.

I stand real still, enjoying the warm and slowly notice the signs of life; quiet sounds of busy; clatter of dishes, bottles in crates being moved about and music—radio maybe—coming up the back stairs.

As you might expect, there's a long, dark-wood bar, beat and scuffed up, running all along the back wall, fronted by —ain't no surprises here—slat-backed, padded leatherette bar stools swivelled towards a wall-hung TV over in the corner. I soon see it ain't the only one in here; there's numbers of them. They're all over the damn place.

I call out towards the sounds of bottles being moved about and after a couple more hollers, a hefty fella in a green Gettin' Lucky in Kentucky t-shirt rolls through the doorway, behind the bar, and wipes his top lip with the back of his hand.

'...do for you?' he says, swallowing the front part of his sentence, and for a moment there I forget what I'm doing here. Or maybe I'm having second thoughts.

Levi tells me he has an opening for evening bar work, which suits me fine, and while he explains how the place works and how much he pays, I try and work out how long it'll take me to earn enough to get my van fixed and move on. I give up after a minute, on account of how Levi calculates what he pays; they got minimum wage here in Kentucky, but, he says, as though I might start reading him my rights, the law says he don't need to pay it if there's tips involved.

'I'll have you working the bar and you're in control, see?' he says. 'It'll incentivise you—you know what that means? It'll incentivise you to be decent to my customers.'

An older woman, beech-nut coloured hair done up like she's going someplace, straightens from over the other side of the bar where she's been setting up a microphone and messing with some tables and chairs.

'The law says,' she calls out, in a friendly voice. 'The law says that if your employees don't make minimum wage with their tips, the employer—that would be you, Levi, honey—the employer needs to make it up.'

She makes her way across the barroom and puts her hand out and I take it in mine. In that instant, I realise I haven't touched another person's skin in months and it pricks at me, almost makes me dizzy. I take my hand back, stroking at it with my other one.

She talks with her hands, and her wrists, loaded as they are with silver and turquoise bracelets, make a fine, jingle-ringing while her hands are non-stop coaxing and shaping the air about her; it's like she's sketching the pictures of what she's saying.

'I don't know you,' she says to me, as though this is a thing of wonder. She looks me over, head to toe and back again and smiles. 'I'm Belle and if you have any questions or suggestions, you just come on over and talk to me.'

She's tall, a big woman, almost looks me right in the eye and it's a real seeing look she gives; I look away. So, this is Belle.

'Is this here your place too, ma'am?' I ask.

'Mercy, no!' She laughs, and I get a flash of a couple gold teeth. 'I have the beauty parlour on Main, that's my baby. But I'm here a good deal of the time, just like everybody else. Levi's is the front porch of our town.'

That makes me smile and she smiles right back. 'Now before you head out, come and help me move these tables and tell me a little something about yourself.' She's turned and walking back to her arrangement.

I look at Levi, wondering if we're done.

'I know better than to get in her way,' he says. 'I'll see you back here tomorrow night, 5pm. Don't let me down.' He rumbles on while he rolls out back and I heft a few tables about for Belle, relieved that her questions about where I'm from and what I'm doing here are easily satisfied by a few general answers.

Heading up from the basement to start my first bar shift, I see the girl, Lark, in the kitchen, scraping food off of a way high stack of dishes and getting to work on them with her bare hands. Steam is clouding up from the sink in front of her. It's hot and the whole cramped-up room is full of noise: radio blaring, machines working and that never-ending TV—there's one in Levi's office, hollering accusations out of the open door. I guess she can't hear that I've stopped on my way upstairs.

She's got her back to me and two things make me stay and look a little longer. She's pulled her sunshine-coloured hair into a top-knot while she works, so I can see right away that she keeps secrets under there; one, she's got herself the shortest buzz-cut I ever seen on a girl, right up to the tops of her ears, dark, like her eyebrows. And two, there's a tattoo curling, delicate and twining up the nape of her neck and behind her ear. I get the strongest urge to get up a little closer and see what it is; words maybe? Flowers on a vine?

She turns to pull a plastic tub full of dirty dishes towards her and the moment she sees me her face breaks into a big, wide smile. A dark flush climbs her throat and spreads out across her cheeks. She looks clean scrubbed.

'Hey, there,' she says and wipes the sweat from her top lip with the back of her hand. 'I didn't see you there.' Her voice carries across the noise, strong and cheerful, but her dark eyes never land for long on mine.

She looks around me, behind me, above my head, catches my eye for a beat—all the while smiling—but then she's back to looking about the place for whatever it is distracting or troubling her. I look over my shoulder, but ain't nobody about but us.

'I'm sorry,' I tell her, realising at last that I'm making her uncomfortable and I turn to leave.

'How are you getting on?' Her arms, which she was holding a little wide of her body, hands flexed open and dripping sudsy water, relax somewhat. She takes a step my way.

I nod and give her a bit of a smile. 'I thought you taught elementary school,' I say, and—bam—feel stupid right away; I sound like I'm accusing her of something.

'I do,' she says. Then she pulls her mouth to one side like she's thinking what to say or how to say it. It brings out a dimple. It disappears the minute she relaxes her mouth, but I saw it for sure and it makes her look less troubled.

'You know...' she tells me after a moment, 'most teachers I know work at least one extra job.'

21

Somehow that gives me a discouraged feeling, I can't say why. Might be because she's got schooling and me, I don't, but here we both are in the same boat? I don't know. So much for The American Dream.

'I help out on my mama and daddy's farm too, you know,' she says, and I nod and try and picture her there, but I don't know what kind of farm it is.

You can see she works hard, though. From them hands all calloused that she plunges bare skinned right into heated water, to the solid kind of way she holds herself. You can see it.

And for all she's a little bitty thing barely comes up to my shoulder, the way she stands there in them rubber kitchen clogs, feet planted, shoulders back, arms held away from her body, if a strong wind came, it don't look like she'd blow over.

2

Well, it weren't what I'd had in mind for myself, that's for sure, but I don't need no body to tell me there are worse places I could have found myself, all things considered. And the truth of the matter is, when I left home in Mama's old camper van, with nothing for company but a six-foot-wide collection of vinyl records, once owned by somebody she called 'your daddy,' the only thing I was thinking was, drive.

TV is permanently on in here and over the past year I been working Levi's bar, it's got so I hardly hear it, despite he likes it up loud. He says it gives the place ambience, which is the longest word ever came out of his mouth, I can tell you. I ain't even certain he knows what it means—kills a mood if you want to know the truth, with all them weather reports blurting out and that never-ending Brooke Adler with her *Random Acts of Kindness* and getting folks to call in and tell her where the do-gooders are now.

But Levi, he don't like the bar to be in silence which, being empty best part of the day it would be. Or so I'm told. Closing my eyes at night is not something I rush into and even when I try it, sleep don't come easy to me, so it suits me just fine that Levi likes to have me on nights. He's old school; thinks that me being a guy adds security to the place.

'Cassidy!' he's hollering at me from other side of the entire room and that's some length. 'I see that suggestions box is spilling its guts again. See that you deal with it, like I pay you to do.'

He's away and through the door that leads down to the kitchen before I finish telling him I'm on it, but he still manages to holler back, 'Then *get* on it!'

He's okay though, Levi, and don't fuss about things that help me out, like paying me cash in hand. I push the suggestions box out of the way; I don't need to read Evangeline's complaints about the wrong pork rinds just now and ain't much I can do about it anyhow, on account of they closed the local Walmart months ago; she's gon have to make do with generic rinds to go with her beer, just like eve'body else.

I settle back into my usual spot behind the bar, with the way-high mirror running right along the length of it to my left and look about the place for who's in tonight. It's a good spot; I see folks come in before they see me.

The door opens and Belle comes in with Beau, arm linked in his and they're laughing, Belle swatting at him and makin like she's gon walk right back out again. Beau, always the gentleman, pulls out a bar stool for her, before he sets himself down in his usual corner seat.

'Look at you like a long-handled broom, propped up there in the corner,' Belle says, arranging herself, then her hair.

This is not a new observation from Belle, but it always makes someone laugh and I don't grudge her that. Lark's right on their heels and shoots me as sweet a smile as always and I'm glad to see it, but for just a twist of a second I'm spooked by the softening it sets off in me and miss the moment to smile back at her.

'Hey, Lark.' I'm already reaching for a glass and shovelling ice into it but I ask her just the same. 'Vodka cranberry?'

'Hey, Cassidy, start me a tab, would you? I'm meeting Evangeline.' She hops up onto a barstool next to Belle, who's giving Beau the long, low-down on something that's evidently bothering her and makes a big old sigh before looking up at the screen above the bar.

'If Ev don't get here soon, she's going to miss tonight's *Random Act of Kindness*.' I roll my eyes at her and she laughs, flushes pink.

'What? It's fun. I love that it's about the kind things people do and *and*,' she stops while I turn the volume up a little on the sound system as the bar fills with a more rowdy crowd. 'I love it because Brooke Adler...' she stops so suddenly I look close at her to see if she's okay. 'She grew up around here, you know.'

She give a look then, hopeful almost, like a child and for the first time since knowing her, I think I see something I never knew till now; Lark has dreams and they're bigger than her daddy's farm and teaching fourth grade at Horse Neck Creek Elementary school. I get a pull of melancholy and almost say, this is it, honey, but I don't have the heart and anyhow, what do I know? Maybe this ain't it for Lark.

When Evangeline finally arrives, smelling of marijuana smoke and axle grease, Lark does like always and says, 'What's the news?'

This kind of gives me a smile on account of there ain't none, mostly. Folks come and go, get drunk, stay sober, fight and fuss, but ain't much of anything you'd call news; this here's a nothing happening kind of town.

'How *are* you, hon?' Belle breaks off from talking to Beau and turns to Ev. 'Did you get my message about the theme for our next Porch Lies?'

'Lord have mercy, you people don't have a single heart between the bunch of you; give a woman a moment to catch her breath, will you?' Ev says, fussing and scooching stools about till she got em just the way she wants them. 'Cassidy?'

'What can I get you, Ev?' I ask, like she don't always have the same thing every time she come in this place.

'Fame and fortune? A little respect?'

I push a bottle of Kentucky Ale over her side of the bar and don't bother with a glass. She settles good on the barstool and takes a long drink.

Right about now is when Evangeline will say something about there ain't never any news anyhow and settle into her own personal commentary on *Random Acts of Kindness* as it plays above her head, but if she do or don't, I miss it tonight because the new waitress has just come on for her shift and she's causing a bit of excitement around here, that's for sure.

First off, she don't talk unless it's something to do with the job. Second, everybody's wanting to know how she coaxes the kind of tips she's getting, out of even the meanest-fisted old farmers and some of your less imaginative folks are wondering if she's turning tricks out back. People sure talk ugly when they see something they want, but can't figure out how to get it.

Thirdly, as she's flying past me, I'm thinking I've seen her some place before, but she's like one a them hummingbirds used to come visit my mama's backyard; just when you think they're going to settle long enough for you to catch a proper look, they're gone and all you see is a kind of buzz of colour, nothing more.

She's disappeared into the back room, tray of drinks held high, and I turn my attention to Belle, who's trying to get her man to agree to play his fiddle at Porch Lies, her monthly story telling jam. She hosts it right here in Levi's, last Thursday of every month, and since I been working here, I've seen it get so there's standing room only, some nights.

'Beau, honey, no one's going to be paying *you* any attention; it's the fiddle they'll be noticing. Folks can get emotional sometimes or lose their train… are you listening to a word I'm saying?' This makes the old fellow tip his hat a little lower over his eyes and chuckle into his glass, not before catching my eye; he's convinced Belle won't rest until she gets the whole town involved; she says community needs work. Belle takes the bait.

'What was *that?*' she asks.

'Nothin at all, Belle, nothin at all,' I tell her and move towards a shout for my attention.

'Oh no you don't.' She leans a little closer, still laughing. 'I know you and that Mona Lisa smile of yours by now.'

'Weren't she a girl?' I ask, not bothering to tell her she don't know me. I open a couple bottles and send them across the bar to a big guy who hasn't took his shades off since he walked in.

'Mona Lisa was no *girl*, Cassidy. I *know* you know a woman when you see one.' She throws a look around no place in particular, but I'm thinking she has somebody in mind.

'You saying I look like a woman, Belle?' I ask, picking up on her Mona Lisa crack.

'Ha!' she laughs and reaches out to pinch at my beard. I flinch my head out of the way, but Belle, she don't take offence and just picks up where she left off.

'No, hon, I am not saying you look like a woman. And don't think I'm not onto you and your evasive ways, young man. You think you can duck and weave until I forget what I asked you in the first place? Though I do ask myself why you want to wear your hair so long, when you have such a fine shaped head. When are you going to get yourself down to my salon and let me give you a decent cut and shave?' She don't wait for my answer, just circles right back to what she wants to know; that's her way. 'Now, what were you and Beau doing with that invisible high five a moment ago? I know you're thinking something when you do that look.'

'What look's that, Belle?'

'Let's just call it "enigmatic,"' she says and takes a drink.

'There ain't no mystery about me, Belle.' I make sure I smile when I say it and push away at my crowding thoughts, while I wipe some spills from the counter.

She shakes the ice in her near empty glass and gives me a nudging look. 'Cassidy?' she's lowered her voice, sounding for the world like she thinks she's my very own mama.

27

'Sweet woman,' Beau cuts in, with a rumble in his chest I know as his most amused laugh. He puts a hand on Belle's powdered cheek. 'We were just laughing at you, is all.'

Belle busts right out with a great whoop of laughter, triumphant. 'I knew it. I *knew* it! You can't put anything past me and don't you forget!' It takes her a moment to ask why, but it don't matter to her one way or another; Belle is more interested in folks knowing there ain't no flies on her.

The next hour or so is a full-on dance and spin with no time for talk, but as is always the way, I hear bits of everything as I move about. I get so the dance I do keeps me somewhere between being there and not. Folks see me, but only when they want to be seen; when they're getting antsy and trying not to show it or admit it even to themselves. They lean forward, push and thrust, find a space between people with their shoulders and hold out a 5 or 10 dollar bill to let me know they want a drink, goddammit.

Folks *see* me only in the space and time they're wanting me, wanting a drink. After that, I disappear to them. They have what they want, they're going to be okay for now. The thing about this is, in the space of one shift, I am by turn king of the coop, everyone calling on me, calling for my attention, trying to come on all buddy-my-pal with me, then faster'n you can blink, they wouldn't pick me out in a line up.

I get to thinking that folks in bars are a little like babies, and what I mean by that is they act like if they don't look at you, you can't see them. This gets me to thinking how it is that evidently they believe that if they're not listening to me, then I ain't hearing them. Folks say a heap of things without giving a thought to what's coming out of their mouth beforehand, nor how loud they're talking. Add liquor to that and, well… you get to see more of them than maybe they'd like in the cold light of day.

The new waitress appearing in front of me, wanting an order filled, snaps me out of my musings. She's standing with all her weight on one hip, head cocked back a little like she's waiting to fire. She slaps down the piece of paper with her pennings across it.

Frozen marg x 2

L.island x 3

Cran.cooler x 1

'Can you read that?' she asks, voice tired and just the wrong side of irritable. This, I'm sure, is on account of my having made her Mojitos x 3 last night, instead of Margaritas x 3 that I'm sure anybody could see was an easy mistake to make; I have not yet met the waiter who writes any better than a doctor scribing for your selective serotonin reuptake inhibitors.

I read it out to her and give her a wink. She nods and turns on her heel.

'So, what do you call yourself?' I ask, stopping her in mid-flight.

All I have to do is look on her badge, which she points out silently, with one quick clack-clack of her nail on the plastic and a look like I'm the town fool.

She turns so quick I have no time to read the badge, but I don't need to; I done it already several times since I first seen her, couple days ago, and I've rolled her name around my mouth getting a feel for it as often as I thought about it.

'Reba?' I say and she turns back, impatient. 'This ain't a bad place to work. Good luck.' I feel stupid the minute the words come out and I don't know what makes me wish her luck, but something softens around her mouth and she nods again before disappearing into the bar room.

At the end of her shift, Reba comes hotfooting up the stairs, stuffing a backpack and loosing her hair from the long, tight braid she wears. She's roughing the fingers of one hand through it like her head aches and her hair, it springs out, alive, red curls lit from behind like a halo. She turns for a split second, and the bar lighting catches her face in a way that—bam—I remember where it is I've seen her before and my belly dives like a busted elevator.

Evangeline and Lark are waiting on me to finish my shift and make me dinner. Once in a while I get a night off, and Lark has made it her business to see I eat a regular meal from time to time. Lark happened to pitch up behind me one night in a local convenience store and like to have a fit right there and then when she saw what I was buying to eat. The only place to buy food in town, now, don't have nothing aside from frozen, canned or packaged goods.

'If you don't eat anything fresh, you're going to become one of the undead, Cassidy.'

I point out to her the impossibility of getting any and she says I should put my name down for the grocery run she and Belle do for folks that don't have access to a vehicle.

'I'm fine, Lark.' She doesn't need to know about where I would put any fresh produce to keep it that way.

While I finish, cashing out for Levi to take over and making sure everything's stocked up, Evangeline is doing her thing. She's peering at her smart phone, scrolling along and calling out to one or other of us to check out the cute toddler stuck in a fold up couch, or a cat says his own name, or some good deed done, filmed and uploaded. She spends so much time looking at that old screen on her smartphone, I wonder how she keeps her auto repair shop open. Maybe she has it projected up onto the wall so she don't miss nothing. This thought gives me a smile.

I'm hunting under the counter for a pen that works when I hear Brooke Adler hollering from above my head, excited as can be, trailing her show. Before I've got my head right side up again, she already repeated the phone number to call for the thousandth time. *'We don't want any good Samaritan to go unrewarded!'* I can hear how wide her smile is.

I grab my coat from under the bar, pat my pocket and jog downstairs to dump my apron in the laundry bin. In ten minutes the three of us head off in Lark's truck, for her place out on her Mama and Daddy's farm, a few miles away.

We're only in her cabin two minutes before TVs on. Lark's in the kitchen finishing a pot roast and green beans. Ev and me, we're drinking beer and sodas, eating nachos from the microwave and in honesty there ain't much difference here than I could be at work, only I get to sit if I want to. I kind of wish I was in my van, just taking it a little easy in the quiet, but there's only so many times I can say no to Lark.

'Don't let me miss the start!' Lark calls out and Ev, by way of reassurance I guess, cranks the volume. I don't know what she's worried about. The show follows the same shape every time anyhow, you seen one you seen a hundred.

Brooke Adler shows a couple uploaded videos people took in the shopping mall or local Walmart and interviews the folks who sent them. She has two faces; excited game show host or I feel-your-pain tell me the juicy bits.

Then there comes a section called Where Are They Now? She follows up on the dude who helped the blind man cross the road, or the lady gave her last twenty dollars to the single mom and ask them how their lives have changed—for the better of course, she ain't interested in them's lives got worse, since she made em recognisable.

Now Brooke Adler's addressing the viewers directly and comes on all excited.

'Now, the bit you all love! We have three new mystery *Random Acts of Kindness* to explore.'

'Did she say "exploit"?' I mutter and laugh aloud as Lark whups me with a pillow.

'What's *wrong* with you?' but she's laughing too and I give her a quick one-arm hug before I get up and move over to the kitchen area to grab me another soda.

'First up,' Brooke is saying. 'Who is this Good Samaritan?' She tells us he's on the right of our picture and that they're going to slow it down so we get a good look at his random act of kindness. 'Take a good look folks,' she says.

True to her word, they slow that thing so it seems to take more time to whip his money out and pay for the family's bucket of chicken than it ever took them to eat it.

'Oh my gosh!' Evangeline is crooning at the TV. 'Look at her face!'

Brooke Adler is talking again. 'Linda Mae wants to thank this kind stranger in person for helping her feed her family when she realised she had lost her purse. So,' the frame freezes on the 'Good Samaritan's' face. 'If anybody out there watching knows who he is, or if this kind-hearted and community minded person is you...' she pauses and flashes a meteor smile at us. 'Well,' she points at the camera. 'You know what to do!'

Ev and Lark are on their third or fourth bottle apiece and chant the lines, along with Brooke as she says them— she don't never deviate—hooting and high fiving each other. You can tell they was in school together and if they weren't well, they shoulda been.

Ticker-taping along the bottom of the screen are the phone numbers to call or text and the faces of the people they want identified frozen just like the mug shots on the local news telling you about another shooting or hold up at a gas station.

'What if he don't want to be found?' I find myself blurting.

The two of them just look at me open mouth like they're a cartoon or something. Then Evangeline reaches for the bag of potato chips I'm holding against my chest and says, 'Why wouldn't he?' like I'm the town fool.

'I can think of a hundred reasons, Ev.'

'Ha! Like what? He's on the run? His wife didn't know he was in that part of town that night?'

I give her a long look, wondering if all her ideas are going to be he's an asshole.

'Maybe, Ev, maybe he just likes his privacy.'

I take myself into the kitchen and regret coming all the way out here dependent on a ride back. I think about the walk without a flashlight on the highway, late at night, and wonder if there's a moon.

'Oh my lor... Is that... Cassidy! Come look at this! Quick!'

I look over at where Lark and Evangeline was lounging. They're both upright and leaning towards the TV.

'What is it?'

Neither looks at me, but Ev says in a voice of wonder, 'Take a look at that and tell me it's not Reba!'

The moment I hear that name, I do not want to look. No. Once you see a thing you can't unsee it, and too many times I've forgot that until it was too late.

But somehow my eyes are focussing on that fuzzing-bright screen and I'm seeing what the girls want me to see and I freeze. I truly do and Lark is saying, 'It *is* her, right?' and I feel I might throw up right there. Lucky for all concerned, it passes before any damage done, but my head is swelling so hot my skull can't contain it and my heart is pulsing so fast, I wonder they can't see it.

Then Lark says my name and nudges at me with her elbow and I see I've walked right over there without noticing. She give me my name again and I don't know what to say, even though I know all she wants is my confirmation of what she sees is true.

She wants me to tell her that yes, that is Reba in that short clip of phone footage, leaning close to a pretty sorry

33

looking fella, all snot and tears and so drunk, he's a disgrace to himself and his whole entire family. Crying, crying, as if he's like to choke to death.

'They'll run it again and maybe we can make out what he's saying,' Lark says and before she's finished speaking it begins again… and again… and over again.

'Don't,' I say, but they ain't paying me any mind, they're so caught up in its being Reba.

'Well, well, well,' Evangeline says. 'The ice queen herself has performed a random act of kindness.'

'Evangeline…' Lark says. 'She's not…' she trails off.

I can't stop staring even though I don't want to look and see Reba's reaching out, putting her arm about him holding him close. I see her leaning close to him, talking gentle, telling him he can take his time. Soft, so soft.

Ev's got her phone out. 'I'm calling in. I never in a million years thought I'd actually know someone. I'm calling in.'

'*No*!' My voice comes out strange and choked and I can see right away that they hear it. They move about, arrange themselves different; Evangeline flips the phone closed and Lark gives a look like, what'd I do?

'Lark,' I say and then I'm lost.

While I'm getting my coat on, I hear Evangeline talkin shit, 'Who'd a thought it? He's obviously got a thing for her.' Lark says something I don't catch and Ev says, 'Well why else would he react that way?'

I come through to the hall where Ev's jangling her car keys and they stop talking and just stare at me. Lark looks at me like she don't know me so well. I try and smile.

'I hate that stuff. Getting in people's business like that. Did anyone ask them if they want to be splashed all over the TV? Now they can't forget even if they want to.'

She looks so hurt and confused that I want to go back and undo it all, but everybody knows that's impossible.

'I never thought of that…' She looks at me real close and strange, like she's seen something that weren't there before and she ain't sure what to make of it yet.

And me, in that moment I am afraid of what all I had that may soon be gone; shelter from the storm.

After Ev drops me, I take my time walking through town, heading home to my campervan and I'm thinking of Reba.

It's a little more'n a year down the road since I last seen her, standing on the steps of the Statehouse, head held defiant. Everybody else there crushed by their pain, heads bowed, each almost hid completely behind the red, person-shaped cut-out they was holding up. I think about how she was stood holding onto the sides of that life-size silhouette, that somebody without a face, without a voice, and it makes me swell inside so bad it aches.

I stop walking a moment and look into the sky, blink against the cold and search for the big dipper. I imagine swinging up there, looking on all this and I feel a little better.

Why I noticed her that day—Reba I mean, I'm not done thinking about her—why I was so drawn to looking at her was because she didn't seem like none of the other left-behind loved ones holding up a cut-out. She was the only one I could see who had that hot wax of anger about her. It was so plain; I wonder that she didn't open her mouth and howl it out at heaven.

That anger tapped me, because all I had been feeling was the weight, the heavy, deadweight of giving up, of my own failure; how I hadn't done the one thing I'd swore to do and so I kind of focussed on her from my place a little to the side of her, like she was the only one still alive. She looked like she was about to take someone out.

I guess it was that about her that stopped folks in their tracks when they started crowding about me, as soon as the whisper went around that I was there. First Lucille, her radar always fine-tuned like I had a tracking device on, hissing out how I should be ashamed to show my face, followed right away by the rest of them, like they'd took to doing, week after dead-end week, since the summer, telling me what a no-good I was. Am.

I take it slow down to the river and enjoy the sound of my feet ringing out and the feel of a mist rolling in. Lark says she gets creeped out when the mist does like that, curling in along the ground when it's dark, but me, I like it; it's peaceful.

I get to Beau's barn, in the field that runs in back of a creek and work at pulling the door open. It hangs low on its hinges, but still fits snug, and there ain't much wind coming through when you close it good. It's cold and still inside, but the smell of hay and straw is clean and reminds me of being a kid and goofing off with my buddies behind Clemson's barn that looks out over the ridge. You could see for miles from it, and there was but one road, led right out towards the mountains and we didn't know where else, and we all used to say, 'There it is, fellas. Road to nowhere!' but that weren't what I was thinking, even then. Nope, I was thinking, I'm gonna find where it *does* go.

Sad to say, when I did finally take the road, I weren't in no fit state to pay any mind to it. Everything happened so fast, without I planned anything, and before I knew what I was doing I'd grabbed a few things and lit out without saying anything to anybody.

I flip the switch, which lights the place with a naked bulb. It might be a little brighter if I would just clean off some of the dust and spider webs, but every time I think of it, it's already too hot to touch. It's way up high and you need a ladder to get to it, which is mighty hard when the bulb blows and it's pitch dark, so I leave it again and tell myself to remember next time I'm here and awake during daylight hours. It gets dark so early, now winters on the way, and often times I'm doing my sleeping when y'all are awake. But I'm not ready to sleep yet.

When Beau and me moved the van in here we stacked bales up and around it for insulation. It works real well and gives me a smile at the same time on account of it resembling a pioneer prairie home. If anybody was to find themselves coming in here, they would maybe take a while to realise it was here at all, which gives me a close approximation of a feeling of security.

I swing open the door of my van, kick my boots off and nudge em under the belly of the bus, then climb on into my home. I always put the bed up when I'm done sleeping. I've got some height on me and like to move as freely as I can in the space I got, so yeah, I fold my blankets, roll my sleeping bag and stow it all away. I know, Mama'd be proud. Anyways, it means that when I get in, I can throw myself on the couch, get myself a drink, work on my drawings or listen to my radio.

I'll get out my inks with their jewel colours and the drabs and greens and look close as I can at a colour plate of Anna's hummingbird or maybe the ruby throated, in *The Birds of America*, and I'll look at the way the feathers are; how they lie, where they join and connect, closer, closer, deeper into what's before my eyes, so I don't keep turning over and over what's gone before.

I read somewhere, or maybe I heard it, I can't recall, that a person don't need to forget everything to survive, just enough, and I wonder what enough might be for me.

Looking at each fine feather I'll get so drawn in I'll forget, for a time, the things that get in the way of surviving. I won't remember swampy heat after a rainstorm that didn't cool nobody, I won't see the orange light of a near-empty parking lot, ground steaming, nor hear yelling voices; I won't remember how slow, how *slow* help is in coming. I'll forget it all. Or enough. Just for a time. I'll keep working at a drawing with those coloured inks until I can't see no more and I know I'll finally be able to sleep a little.

Beau lets me use his postal address, so I can send away for them mail order on account of there being no store in town that sells much of anything besides cattle feed and workwear and the only paints you'll find are at the hardware store or at Belle's beauty parlour.

He gives me shit when a parcel comes. 'You spend all your money on art supplies,' he tells me. 'It isn't a wonder that you can't raise the money to fix your van.'

But I know he don't grudge me and little by little, since I come here, I been breathing out... waiting a spell... breathing out a little more.

I made him a painting of a grayling, which is a fish he talks endless about and is real pretty, if you want my opinion. He was tickled to bits that I'd managed to find the right shade of blue and keeps it propped on the dash of his truck.

But tonight, I don't go near my paints. As soon as I'm inside my van, I flip on the heater and get the place started on warming up before I take my coat off and while I'm waiting on that, squat and reach under the bench.

Long ago, before I was what Mama called her career break, they built storage in this van for the vinyl they collected to be stored the right way up. They're pressed together with the intention of preventing warping and I think pretty much it's worked, but I can't be sure. I mean to get me something to play them on some day.

Mama says she and my Daddy, spent a lot of time on the road, travelling from one record fair to another in between festivals where she played and sang with her guitar, songs she wrote on the road. And she always talked about him like he was something special. But I always wondered, if he was so great how come he upped and left her with a baby in her belly and no forwarding address?

I pull out a shoebox from under the bench and lay it on my lap, but my breath does like a mayfly on the surface of a pond and I think maybe I'll just put it right away again without looking inside. I don't need no news clipping to tell me what I already know, but Reba's doing such a fine job of not knowing me, I keep doubting myself.

It takes me a little while to find what I'm looking for once I open the box, on account of letting my eyes wander over the other clippings and photographs that rise up towards me first. I try not to look too close at some of what I keep in here and I wonder why I keep it, if I ain't never gon look at it.

Then, my fingers come on the stiff bend of plastic on the smallest little hospital bracelet I ever saw. I can't look at that now. I know what it is just by feel and push it down the side, tucking it in alongside the other one.

It took my breath and I take a minute before I try and come back to this van, this barn. I shouldn't have opened the box, but then Reba comes into my head with her long, red braid, her angry face and those eyes full of everything, all of it, aching and hurting, and I remember why I'm in this stupid box.

I turn up a clipping from the Mountain Herald that makes my stomach rise and meet my throat. I do not want to read it. I can't, though truth be told I could recite every word that's printed there. I put it away and pick up another. This one, this here, is the one I'm hunting.

Frankfort KY
More than 100 people gathered on the steps of the Statehouse on Thursday to remember the 43 people killed by their spouses, partners and exes in Kentucky last year.

At the 17th annual Silent Witness Ceremony, KY. Attorney General Wilson Roberts read the names of the 34 women and 9 men killed, and a brief description of each slaying. Survivors, law enforcement officers and other volunteers held life-size cutouts—red for women, blue for men—representing each victim. A purple cutout stood in for the unknown victims of domestic violence.

And there she is, right there at the edge of the photograph, her crazy curls blowing in the wind, real wild. If she didn't keep it so tight and braided at work, I might have recognized her sooner.

It's some days before Reba's working again. She looks like she hasn't slept in days and for some reason I want to tell her I know how that feels.

'I seen you before,' I tell her before I can think if it's a good idea or not.

'I seen you too.' She quirks that one eyebrow. 'Every time I come in this place, there you are. Don't you ever take a night off?' She's tapping hard at her tray with her pen and waiting on me to finish pouring out a root beer.

'What would I do with a night off?' I say, and smile at her.

She don't get within a five mile radius of smiling back and I'm puzzled, I truly am. 'How come you're so hard on me?' I ask and for a minute there, she looks surprised, but then it's flown.

'I treat you same as everybody else.'

'But I ain't everybody else.' Which, truth be told, feels a stupid thing to say the moment it comes from my mouth and I'm ashamed by my own self. I wish I could say it, *I seen you soft*, but I'm afraid she'll take it wrong.

'What makes you think you're different to everybody else?' she snaps her question at me and spins around at the bell telling her that there's a grill order up.

I feel a deep sigh pulling its way through me and wonder why I keep acting like such a dumb ass smart Alec around her. It's like I've worked out how to make sure she don't ever take me serious and I'm running with it.

40

Beau's voice interrupts my reverie. "'Don't blame me,'" he reads slow and clear. "'I voted for the American.'"

He's looking over my shoulder at a bumper sticker Levi put up on the mirror behind the bar a few days ago and I can only assume is in reference to our 44th president of these United States. I don't like it, but what can I do? It ain't my bar and in point of fact, this here is a red state, so no doubt all them people, some of who I'm happy to call friends, probably just think that bumper sticker is a hoot and agree with it anyhow. The old fellow catches my eye and chuckles soft and there's a watery look in his eye that makes me sad.

'I like to think we're all Americans,' he says, then gives me what I take to be a hopeful look and says, indicating the sticker, 'I imagine that has nothing to do with you?'

I don't answer, I don't need to, and I pour him his second and last Wild Turkey of the night. He don't deviate from that ever, not in all the time I known him.

'There are two kinds of people in this world, boy, them that knows their limits and them that don't!' he says. Amen to that.

I start fishing around in my pocket.

'What do you have for me?' he asks.

'Now, *why* you think I have something for you, I do not know.' And his face makes me laugh aloud. 'Here y'are,' I tell him, and I pull out the prettiest three feathers, marked and marbled with brown and black and white—white like clouds you see setting over the mountain tops in springtime.

'Much obliged.' He opens the toolbox he always has set up on the bar beside him. He don't go nowhere without it and keeps all his fixings for making fishing flies stored there.

The door opens, bells ring and Beau grows three inches when he sees who it is.

'Good evening y'all!' Belle is wrapped up good in a bunch of scarves and what looks like all everybody else's coats besides. She comes with her arms held out. 'Did anybody take a call from KYTV today?'

If Ev and Lark's heads was on a string together, they couldn't have swung them better.

'What?'

Belle got what she wanted and gives me a wink.

'I had an email at the centre asking for a tour of our community. Brooke Adler is doing a new show about the reality of rural living in America and she'd like to start with us.'

I hadn't planned on going to the Silent Witness ceremony —I didn't even know there was such a thing. Every year. That's quite a thought. Every year.

If I hadn't of seen it on a TV in the bar I was sitting in, I probably would never have known. I didn't even know that's where I was headed as I walked out the door; it just came up in front of me. I turned the corner and there it was already underway, a funeral-silence hanging over the small crowd as the bell chimed and another woman's name was read out.

I remember someone coughing and it sounding so small and lonely out there in the open, until a cough from somewhere close by answered it and papers fluttered, feet shuffled before the silence returned. I remember how at first everybody there seemed alone, staring straight ahead or head bowed, until it came clear to me that something connected one to another; a tilt of the head, the closeness of a shoulder; folks with an arm about each other or a hand being held.

That's when I saw Reba for the first time and somehow realised that she was as truly alone as I; the only person there not being held or holding, in some small way, another human being.

I fixed my eyes on her, anchored myself to her, trying not to get crushed by the weight of the most god-awful feeling of lost, aloneness, scared I might howl my insides out, listening as one name after another was read out.

It was late fall, coming into winter and what a winter: ice storms, snow-fall and blizzards like I'd never seen; north-eastern weather, not Kentucky as I'd known it. But nothing was as I'd ever known it anymore, so it didn't surprise me as it might have done.

Lark and me walk down dark unlit streets. There's a few streetlights placed here and there, but the county can't afford to light much, so there it is. It's almost 6 o'clock and getting colder by the minute. Lark puts her gloved hand through the crook of my arm and shivers hard.

'I can't get my head around Brooke Adler coming here,' she says. 'I spoke to her myself this morning.'

I know this already on account of it being the main topic of conversation all day from anybody caught my ear. 'Is that right?' I say, as easy as you like.

'She called the community centre, personally. Not even an assistant or anyone. I think that tells you a lot about... Cassidy?' she halts, looks at me, then carries on like she means business. 'I know you think it's a load of...'

'You got that right,' I tell her, lickety split.

'*Stop!*' She laughs and pulls my hooked arm close to her. 'So cynical! Were you born like this? Did you come slouching out of your mama with that wrinkle in your forehead and one eyebrow raised?'

I'm surprised by the sudden sadness that causes me. No. No I was not always like this. I pat my pocket, tap-tap. 'Go on,' I say. 'Tell me. What is so appealing to you about having a TV show circus come to town?'

Lark makes a huffing like she's getting tired of this, but good-natured enough, she presses on, 'It could actually be really good for our little town.'

'How so?'

'Well, if we raise our profile in a positive way, we might attract funding or sponsorship to help with our community programmes.'

There's a strong voice in me wants to ask who gave her that idea, but she goes on. 'Brooke Adler,' she takes a breath. 'Brooke was telling me. That you can't buy the sort of publicity that you get being featured in shows like hers and businesses like to be associated with good causes, American values, that kind of thing.'

We're almost at the community centre, which is where we've been headed, behind Lark's church. Yeah, I volunteer at the food bank and soup kitchen couple times a month, but I have a mind to try going on a Sunday maybe soon. I'm not averse.

'I know you're one of the good guys, Cassidy,' she tells me, and I feel hot around my neck. 'For all your cynicism. It's not everybody who'd do this you know.'

'Well,' I say. 'There but for the grace of god.'

What I don't say is what's in my heart; that I remember the day I met her like it was yesterday and that if she ever wants me to do something for her, I'll do it.

Lark is continuing to talk up a storm beside me, and I've kind of lost the thread on account of following my own thoughts.

'Lark,' I say.

'I'm doing it again, aren't I?' she says, stopping and looking up at my face. 'Just jibber jabbering, I'm sorry.' She's laughing, but I feel bad about her thinking that's why I cut in like that.

'Naw, Lark,' I say, wanting to make her feel better about herself. 'You're alright, I was just thinking.' We walk on. 'What do you make of Reba?' I can't help it.

'Oh.' That's all she says. 'Oh.' like that. 'You were thinking about Reba?'

The way she says it makes my thoughts crowd in a corner and huddle. I don't feel like talking no more.

'She's had hard times, I think, don't you?' and she sounds sweet and sincere, like always.

'I guess so,' I say and that's it. We're at the back door, which is cracked a little open with steam and warm smells coming out.

'Ready to spread a little comfort?' she asks and in we step.

The heat and noise kind of whaps you in the face after the cold and the smell, it takes me back; steaming-hot, roasted squash.

Mama grew any number of varieties in the yard, and the kitchen back home smelled of it, and hot buttered corncobs, all summer and into fall. I used to tie the long sharp-haired vines onto the porch rails and let the sun dry the fruits and thicken the skin, so they'd store through the winter.

I follow Lark as she pushes through too many people who shouldn't have to be here. There's easily close to a hundred bodies, not counting the twelve volunteers, and every time I arrive it seems it's more crowded. Tonight, on account of the freezing weather I guess, there's more folks pushing against each other for a plate of hot food than I ever saw.

'My folks are doing just fine, Mister Ray,' Lark is telling an old fella with yellow eyes like a sick dog. 'They said to say hey, next time I saw you.'

Lark tells me she often sees folks who worked her mama and daddy's farm over the years and they always want to be remembered to them.

'Just about breaks my heart to see a man like him so broken down,' she says, heading for the storeroom out back to stow our coats. 'Worked hard all his life and wiped out by chronic illness. His wife died last fall and he hasn't been the same since.'

Now this place here don't just dish out hot food, there's a food pantry that the church puts together too. Sometimes I'm in there filling boxes for folks to take home, other times like tonight, I'm out front.

I haven't been dishing up macaroni and cheese for more than maybe ten minutes when glory be, if it ain't Reba her own self walking into the room. She comes in proud, head up and holding a little boy who's squinting in the bright lights, looking like he just woke up and he's landed somewhere he ain't none too sure about. He presses in right close to her side and I have to breathe a little more careful when I see her hand and how it just floats down and touches his cheek, draws him nearer until he's under her wing.

'Uh, whenever you're ready...' A young fella about my age is looking at me like, the-fuck's-your-problem, and I give him my full attention and serve him and tell him I'm sorry for the delay, but he's muttering about kicking a man when he's down and giving me the evil eye. I don't grudge him. There but for... you know what I'm saying?

I look over at Reba again and she sees me. Her face just kind of falls to pieces before she pulls it back together. She looks so tired too, like she might just stop where she is, right there.

Well, I know it's stupid an all, but when I see that look on her face, I get a hopeless feeling. She don't smile nor make any sign of recognition, save from the wholesale dislike of my being there and I think, Well that's okay, who of any of us want to see a dude from work at the food bank? Might be it would be a little better if I was standing in line with her, but serving out hot meals to the destitute?

I don't think so. Yeah, that's what I'm thinking. But I'm feeling sad and stupid and in the way.

I am minded that the line is building and getting restless, so I get to it and next I look up, she's gone. I feel real uneasy then and look about quick, for someone who can take my place. It's crowded and busy and I'm hunting with my eyes for anyone wearing the green volunteer T shirt, someone who might free me up to go and search out Reba. I can't stand to think she might have turned tail on account of my being in the place she least expected. I check the time. At last I spot Lark, busy accompanying an elderly looking fellow into the storeroom and helping him fill a grocery bag with his most pressing needs. I holler her name across the hall above everybody's heads, hoping it carries above the noise. She turns to me and looks. 'What is it?'

'I need to step outside for a minute,' I tell her when she gets close and I don't even wait for her affirmative. I'm out, before she can open her mouth.

The door bangs behind and it's quiet as the grave and cold as one too. It don't take me but seconds to see that ain't nobody on that long, lonely street; not this way nor that. There's a thick snow falling, but it must not have been when she took flight at sight of me. How do I know that? Well, a little ways down the street is two sets of footprints, marking the snow, appearing out of nowhere, like they two flew out of the church and landed light on the ground. A great loneliness comes on me.

'Cassidy?' It's Lark at my side and she asking me what all's the matter.

'Did you know she was a mama?' I ask, still looking down the street, like as if they might appear from somewhere just as easy as they disappeared.

'Who?'

'Reba,' I answer and feel Lark shrink a little from my side. 'She come in with a little boy and lit outta there just as soon as she laid eyes on me.'

'Oh.'

Then I make myself laugh. 'You ain't scared of me, Lark?'

She laughs with me and the way she sounds, makes me smile for real, like always and without thinking on what she might make of it, other than what I mean, I say, 'You wouldn't run out on me, would you?'

'No,' she says, and I feel a momentary unease by how serious she looks at me. 'No, I wouldn't.'

'I have to get going,' I say truthfully, and I ask if she has someone to walk back with. In actual fact, she tells me, she has a ride, which makes me feel a whole lot better on account of it getting colder by the minute.

Then something happens I swear to god I did not plan. Inside as I'm fumbling in the storeroom for my coat and rucksack, putting my hat on, good and low over my ears, I notice no one is about. In all this crowded, busy place, ain't no one here with me, which I'm telling you is got to be a first. Everybody's got their eyes someplace else and I think, well, she would've gotten a bag of her own, only I put a stop to it on account of being me. And I think about that youngin she had with her, scared and tired and no doubt hungry and I grab me as many of them jars and cans as I can without too much thinking getting in my way and I'm out of there and on my way back towards the centre of town before I can think on it any more.

So, she's a mama. Reba is somebody's mama, a little boy. This is the thought that keeps time with me on my night-run back to work—I ain't one for being late, it gives you no slack for when you might need it—and besides, getting some speed on keeps me warm. The thought of Reba begins to run itself ragged around my head as I jog, my breath coming hard now and the cold burning the inside of my nose, my throat swelling dry.

48

The snow's falling thick and I just love the quiet it brings. I keep to the salt and grit on the middle of the road before it gets a little too busy with slow-creeping cars, the snow chains on all them tyres making a particular kind of muffled-crunch sound. I slow up and jump over the black-pitted snow, piled high along the sidewalk, pass the Paws For Thought pet parlour and Belle's Beauty shop all shut for the night hours ago. I try not to think too much, but I'm having a hard time figuring why it should have such a hold on me; Reba having a kid, I mean. I find myself wondering who the daddy is and if he's around. And then, way down in the pit of my belly, a hard twist of something that I have no words for comes on without warning.

I'm away from the broken part of town now and turn onto Main street, hugging lit-up shop fronts as I move along, as though the light coming from the glass fronts are going to warm me like a fire might.

Finally, I slow, turn left off Main and follow the road towards the vacant lot. Next to it is the only building still standing at this end of the street. Folks here tell me they'd started to redevelop the area, when the banks crashed; Levi's, facing the wrecking ball one day, was spared it the next.

The door swings open as I get to it and the light coming out somehow surprises me more than its bang. I recognise the country music that don't get played too loud and the roll-on rumble of talking and calling out; the sound of the TV. I take in a last pull of that cold night air, and hot to sweating under my down coat, pulling at my muffler and hat and calling out hello to all the folks, I put a smile on my face and head on to another night working the bar.

I'm chewing on the problem of Reba's kid going hungry; it's preying on me something awful. So much that it takes me a moment to notice ol' Beau leaning toward me with one of his looks like, 'I have something to tell you and you are going to want to hear it.'

I should probably say right off he's never wrong. When he gets to giving off that look, I *know* I'll want to hear what he has to say.

It's still early enough in the evening to be a little quiet and Beau's just not one of them fellows that make you wish you was running your ass off just so's you can get away from his talk. He's like the wise man; speaks because he has something to say, not because he wants to say something.

So he gives me the look with his black eyes a little crinkled and them bushy white eyebrows raised into his hat band, but before I can get my slouch good and relaxed, the door busts open like gunshot, which never fails to make me lose a beat, and in come a bunch of out-of-towners who don't look like they're holidaying. There's something too tight, too alert about the woman in front of the three guys who come crowding in with her; she looks like she's casing the place, but trying not to show it. She's got a big platinum-gold smile, but it can't seem to make the climb up to her eyes, which are snapping about the bar while she talks out of her smile at the guy to her left. He's looking all over too, and they make a beeline for me and what I have racked up behind me. I nudge myself away from Beau and make sure they see how glad I am that I might get to fix them a drink.

Up close, the woman looks like she works out too much and eats too little, all wire and sinew and nerves and she reminds me of one of them reporters on TV. She presses against the bar and puts her hands down, splat, on the wood and gives me a fine view of almost every one of her 500 dollar-a-piece teeth. Then I realise, hot damn, she *is* one of them reporters on TV and not just any old one. It's Brooke Adler her very own self. I throw a look in Beau's direction and see from the secret smile running all over his face that he was fixing to tell me something about this.

'What can I get for you today?' I ask the woman.

Right about now, the fellows she came in with kind of flank her like they're her bodyguards and one of them's got her back too. They're smiling at me like, 'hey, hey we're all buddies here already! Isn't that neat?' I'm used to that; everybody wants to be your friend before you've served em.

I play along, answering their questions about local micro-breweries and trying to work out if they're trying to catch me out for a fool who has no business behind a bar, or if they really don't know the difference between an open fermented beer and a closed, or what IPA stands for. And see, the reason this bothers me, is this: guys like that, they don't usually go in for showing their ignorance. Mostly they'll be telling you how *much* they know, even if they don't know shit. So, me, I'm on alert.

'Brooke,' says one of the guys to the TV girl. He's tall and a little stoop shouldered, like he's not used to fitting through doorways, or gained his height too young and real fast and is still expecting someone to make a joke about the weather up there. 'What're you drinking?'

She swings her hair, looks toward Beau who's working on one of his fishing flies.

'Now that,' she says, like she just spied a log fire all lit up on a cold day, 'looks very good.'

But she's looking at his glass of Wild Turkey and I'm right away thinking, lady there is no way you're a bourbon on the rocks kind of girl, why you want to kiss up to Beau like that? It won't work anyhow. He's no one's fool, that one.

She cocks her head a little bit, kind of like a fancy breed dog and says, 'You know? I think I'll just stick to what I know. Give me a Jack Daniels and Coke.'

Her eyes are blue and wide and I'm sure she knows they're pretty. The guys order bottles of our local bottled ale and settle in, breathe out and loosen their collars and all of that.

'So,' I say, as I'm whappin' down coasters in front of them. 'What brings you into town?'

Brooke laughs and dips her head, raising her eyes up to look at me.

'Oh dear...' and she laughs again, inviting me to laugh with her at whatever minor foolishness she's guilty of. 'Is it that obvious we're out-of-towners?'

I glance lickety-split around the barroom and then give her a look.

''Fraid so. We don't get too many types like you in here. I hope you're not trying to pass under the radar. It's already way too late for that.'

She laughs and tells me, 'We're from KYTV. You probably know my show, Brooke Adler's *Random Acts of Kindness*?'

She says it like there ain't no way, no how I'll tell her no, and Lord knows I wish I could, just to see that look on her face change. But she knows and I know I can't; that very channel is blaring above our heads waiting to call me a liar.

So instead I just give her a long, slow, let's move on kind of look and she takes her cue, but she looks as though she doesn't really believe I'm uninterested, because it's everybody's life's ambition to be on TV, it's what everyone wants, right?

'When you're ready!' Fella's voice, friendly enough hollering over the noise, calls my attention and I nod his way to show him, I seen you. I slap and slide coasters down, and drinks, start to take money and make change, all before you can make up your mind between a Sol or a Corona.

It's right about three hours after I lifted the groceries from the storeroom and they're playing on my mind. Not, you understand, because I feel any too bad about it, but more on account of my not knowing how I'm going to get them to Reba and her little boy. I can picture the look on her face if I were to stroll up to her with a bag of charitable donations and I'm telling you, it gives me a real feeling of uneasy just thinking about it.

'What'll you have?' My eyes are on the friendly sounding dude, but I have to ask him to repeat himself, which is not a thing I usually need to do.

'Still snowing out there?' I ask, as I top his bottle of Coors. We both know the answer, but something about the expecting smile leads me to believe he's the sort to want a little small talk and I ain't one to grudge that.

'Sure is and temperature dropping by the minute,' he tells me.

'You from outta town?' This being another question I know the answer to.

'Yep. Got in yesterday. I'm camera crew on the Brooke Adler show, we're filming a piece for...'

'Cassidy! I'm dying of thirst here!' I see a twenty-dollar bill flapping about and turn more fully toward it, glad not to have to hear about that carcase-picking, buzzard of a show.

'All you folks are payin' with money,' I say. 'So that had better be my tip!' I can talk that way, on account of the holder of that twenty is known to me. 'You be sure to wrap up warm when you're done here,' I tell the TV fella. 'People been known to freeze to death when they get a couple drinks inside of them.' I look back to the hopeful owner of the money. 'What'll you have, Freak?'

Lark just about dies every time we give him that name, but that's how he calls himself. I'd been working here three months before I knew he *had* another name. Lark is the only person I know of who calls him by Bill. I like to tease the two of them that she thought of the dullest of names as a protest. Of course, I ain't a fool and know right off that his mama never gave him the name of Freak on his joyous arrival, but it didn't interest me to ask. The way I see it, folks just want to be who they say they are; ain't my business messing with that.

'Cassidy, I want you to make me a very strong rum and Coke and I want you to tell me where in high water *that* came from.' He's pointing over my shoulder at the long, tall mirror that give me eyes in the back of my head.

Now Freak, he owns a ol' timey music store in town. It's the kind a place you can flip through racks of vinyl records and buy a guitar should you be minded to, but is so down on its luck on account of nobody having a buck to spare for a record they don't own a player for that he travels a lot to fairs and suchlike, looking for a gem nobody else spotted. And here's the thing; I was so bent on providing an antidote to Levi's bumper sticker perpetuating the lie that our president is not born on US soil, that I omitted to think about the repercussions of re-igniting his interest in my vinyl collection. I turn to look at the *Kate Smith Sings... We're All Americans* 78 I stuck up there earlier.

'Nothin' to do with me,' I say, looking about for somebody who needs me. I catch Beau's twinkle and enjoy the moment of understanding that passes between us. He's shaking his head a little and chuckling at me.

'That caught my eye too.' TV guy has joined us, sidled along the bar to get him some company. 'Who's the collector?'

'Nobody,' I say.

'Cassidy, here,' Freak says at the same time and points me out, no room for compromise.

TV laughs. 'Well,' he says, looking first at him and then me. 'This is what you might call A Situation!'

Freak goes on, 'He has a vinyl collection as long as this counter top.' He's talking bar talk now—it ain't nearly that big. 'And try as I might, I can't get him to let me take a look at it.'

'So how do you know I warn't just talkin' big when I told you about them vinyls?' I ask, hoping he'll drop it.

Everybody laughs but Freak, who says, 'Well...' before he too lets out one hell of a laugh and says, 'You got me there. Maybe I was just taken in by the bragging of a little man.'

Now Freak, he's a big fella and even though I got some height on me, he's a head above *and* some, so it ain't as though I'm like to be offended by his comment. We all do the laughing he wants but I feel his sharp edge and I see he is sore that I'm holding out on him.

TV guy speaks up now, 'What age are you, uh...' he's fishing for my name. 'Cassidy?'

I give him a look for a while. Name and Date of Birth can make me nervous these days.

'Old enough,' I say. I don't ask him his years, on account of it don't interest me. Anyhow, any fool with eyes can see he's sliding towards his half century. 'Is it important?' I ask just for something to say.

'It's of interest,' he replies and goes on fast. 'Only because I love to hear of a young person with an interest in vinyl. It's a particular love of mine and I often find myself getting into... discussions, shall we say?' We all laugh for him. 'About the superior nature of a vinyl recording. How did you become interested?'

'I'm not.' I disappoint him with my lie. 'It's just something my old man left behind.'

As the night wears on, I get more and more itchy trying to figure out what to do about Reba missing out on her food. So much, to the point I'm beginning to hallucinate her going hungry and her little boy crying his self to sleep and all on account of me.

I'm helping the last die-hards to remember which way the door opens and sweeping up the mess they all dropped under the tables, when I see what it is I need to do, to fix what I done.

Brooke Adler and her crew are still talking in a cluster by the pool table and taking their sweet time and I'm feeling that wrench and twist inside, comes when you're thinking fast, and the world acting slow.

'I'm a have to hurry you now, folks,' I say, making sure I don't make eye contact; they're more likely to leave if you don't, I have found. 'Fun's over for tonight. See you again.'

'Oh, you get on,' Brooke Adler says, easy and like she's old friends. 'We'll see ourselves out.'

As though she wants to prove she's good as her word, she starts to hustle her crew. Now I know this is against rules, but Levi's out by the dumpster and I see I might miss my chance if I don't do it now.

'Come on guys, we don't want anyone to get a bad impression of us, do we?' Brooke flashes me a smile.

As soon as she turns to the door, I hot foot down the back stairs, look about me for where Levi's at, just in case he's beat me to it and seeing all clear, slide as quick and silent as I can into his office. My blood rushes and pumps in my veins, my heart pulsing so loud in my ears as to make them unlikely to hear anything and I'm jumpy as a long tailed cat in a room full of rocking chairs; if he catches me here, I ain't got no job come tomorrow.

I know what I'm hunting but uncertain where I might find it and for a moment I just stand, froze to the spot. Time's a wasting. There's a pile of papers on Levi's desk and I scrap through them, but they're all delivery notices and bills. Now what? I start to think what a damn fool I'm being, he's like to have all his employee records on his computer and I get an uneasy feeling, now my first impulse has died, that there's something kinda wrong in what I'm doing. Just as I'm deciding on giving up and facing Reba like a man, I notice one of them rolodexes and I get a lift to my spirits. All I want to do is fix what I done. My fingers are just about managing to flip their way through the index cards, when the door slams open against the wall and it's Levi hollering at me, 'What in hell are you doing in my office?'

I freeze. What the hell *am* I doing in here? I want to just fess up and tell him the truth, but I don't want to put

Reba's private business about the place. I'm in a tight spot for sure and I ain't never been any good at lying; I'm a tongue biter, always was until the one time it really mattered, then I'd have bit my tongue right out there and then if it would've made a difference.

'Levi,' I say, stumbling over my words, colouring up hot. 'I apologise for coming in here. I was just...'

He looks at my hands shoved in my pockets. 'You want to show me what's in your pockets?' His voice tells me I got no choice, but I try just the same.

'I wanted to uh... I was meaning to...' and I see that I can't say anything without making it a thousand times worse.

'Don't make me have to turn your pockets out, Cassidy.'

Well that works and I pull out the hand with the card from the rolodex, before I pull out my other hand after a quick tap-tap on my box. He don't need more'n a second to see what's what. For a flick I see a sort of disappointment in his eye and I feel worse.

'Are you kidding me? You're sneaking about snagging female employees home addresses? I should fucking fire you on the spot! I never would have expected...' he's shaking his head and I can see I've put him in a difficult position.

'Levi, I didn't mean no harm. I swear to god it ain't how it looks, I just weren't thinking...'

'Damn right, you weren't! Not okay. Jeez...' He looks real uncomfortable, scratching his stomach, hanging out over the belt of his blue jeans. 'I don't know...'

I can see he don't really want to let me go; it would be hard to find someone else who don't mind the long, late nights. And he likes me, in as much as Levi likes anybody.

'I don't know...' he says and scratches at that ol' belly of his again, before he looks around the room like it's gon tell him what to do.

'It won't happen again, Levi,' I say. 'I was trying to return something belonged to her and she ain't been in work, so I... it was stupid.'

'Trying to return something, huh?' he's curious now, not as angry. But he still don't quite know what to do; knows what he *should* do, but don't really want to have to.

'I understand if you need to fire my ass, but I really need this job.'

'Everybody needs a job, Cassidy. There's nothing special about you.'

We stand there watching each other. I'm holding my breath hoping he's gon come down on my side, saying nothing until finally he lets out a big breath.

'Okay...' he says. 'I'll keep you on for now, but if you pull any more stunts like this, you're out, no excuses. Out. You understand?'

'I sure do. Appreciate it, Levi.'

'But I'll be talking to Reba, see if she has any issues with you, you got that? Now get your ass out of here.'

I do just that, but I walk whap, right into that Brooke Adler, who's looking straight at me and she says, 'Oh! I am so sorry I was looking for the restroom?'

'All the way down here?' I say, before I can think. She keeps looking at me, close and an expression starts to show on her face like something's unfolding in her mind and spreading out to be looked at.

'Have we met before?' she asks and I shake my head, relieved, knowing for sure we haven't. But then she slays me.

'You remind me of... so familiar... I wonder what you'd look like after a haircut and shave?'

I hustle her out, telling her even my own mama don't know that, laughing with her, sweating a little with nerves, but it's only when I'm halfway down Main street I wonder what she heard between me and Levi.

Out in the cold I pat at my pocket like I always do and write Reba's address on my hand, so I don't forget it; I'm rattled and don't want to make a mistake. Reba's gave her address as one of the condos over near the elementary school and I head that way with my package of food, hoping there's somewhere safe I can leave it; she ain't the only hungry person in town.

I pick up a can of Spaghetti O's here, a package of macaroni there and take a detour by her house after work whenever I can. It becomes part of my routine to swing wide through town and take in the dark streets by the school, drop some food on her porch and head on down towards the creek and home. I could be doing a paper route, I'm so quick about it, but tonight, I find myself just standing there on the top step to her porch and I can't move on.

I'm thinking about that little boy, his head under Reba's cradling hand and I can't stand how sad it makes me. His hair was so bright, it put me in mind of my little brother. I wonder what his name is and where his daddy is.

I've taken out a box of Hamburger Helper and I'm wondering if she could use it and there's a package of Moon Pies too; little kids love them. I'm thinking maybe I'll just leave the loaf of bread and the peanut butter and grape jelly, when the door clicks and opens a crack.

'*What do you want?*' Reba's voice comes, low and strangled, like she's wanting no one to hear but me. She's scared or angry or both, I can't be certain, but that don't surprise me—many's the time I've screwed up, confusing the two. I put my hands out, opened up, trying to show her I don't mean nothing, but my insides are roiled up, a boiling sea, and I want to turn right around without another word and leave her alone. I don't want her to be thinking ill of me. I don't want her frightened by me, but right about now

I'm seeing that things ain't looking too good. I feel the weight of the groceries in my pack and remind myself of why I came, but I'm rooted, my mouth shut down.

'It's you, isn't it?' she says, without moving to open the door any further. For a flash, I wonder if she's remembered, but she goes on. 'It's you that's been leaving food by my door.' The way she says it, you'd think it's skinned rabbits I been leaving there. I nod and try and explain, but she goes on. 'Come on out of the shadows.'

I take a step or two, my boots shuffling on the grit-salted porch and I'm feeling like I'm a kid been busted. It's then I hear a clicking and my insides move upwards in a rush and hover. I keep real still and try and breathe steady.

'Are you cocking that thing or standing it down?' I ask her.

I see her reach to her side and lay the pistol down and when I breathe out again, my belly trembles and I recognise the feeling for what it is. Don't believe anybody tells you they ain't scared when somebody's pointing a gun at them; they're either lying or dumb-ass stupid.

'Reba,' I say. 'I'm real sorry I snuck about, but…'

'You should be.' She says, sharp and snappy. 'No buts. You just should be.'

For some reason, this makes me smile. I guess it's the no fooling way she says it. 'You're right. No buts. I'm sorry.'

'This is not a funny thing.' She says the word funny like she's slamming on it, *bam!* 'Don't you laugh at me.' She's real fierce and I feel even worse, if that's possible. But then to my surprise, she looks at me a little softer and seems to be trying to decide something. 'Cassidy,' she says, and I near enough keel over right there on the porch, because she said my name. She actually said my name. In all the time we been working in the same damn bar, while she's been sassing or ignoring me, she has never not once give me my name and it has bothered me and bothered me. Because we shared something, she and me, and she don't acknowledge it and I know it's partly this that's been chewing me up inside.

'Yes, *Reba*,' I say back at her and I can see a sweet flash of humour in her eyes that she covers up fast. She shakes her head a little then looks real sober.

'Cassidy, you are one ignorant man if you don't understand that it is *never* okay to follow a woman without her knowledge and sneak about her home.'

I hate the way that sounds, but all I can say is, 'I didn't want you to miss out because of me.'

She gives an irritable shake of her head, like she's swatting away a horsefly and says, 'What are you talking about?'

'I saw you there, Reba,' I tell her, soft. 'At the food bank.' She raises herself up a little taller. 'With your little boy...' She jerks her chin out in front and gives me a look like right then, she despises me. I go on but then stop, because her eyes are filling with tears.

She steps back and shuts the door, and the worst of it is she don't even slam it, she just quietly backs up and pushes it silently closed and I'm left standing, with all her despising and plenty of my own, crowding and pressing about me.

After a little while, her home staying dark and silent, I take my backpack off and leave the food on the mat. I'm worried about the cardboard packages of macaroni and cheese getting damp and spoiling, so I take the hood off my jacket and wrap them in it, before heading back the way I came.

When I arrive at work next evening, two things. One, I find my hood on a shelf behind the bar and Reba's scrawl on a tore off piece of notepad—*Thank you*. And two, Brooke Adler is back in and has a group of regulars around her, talking and laughing like they's old friends. She's got

Evangeline and Lark up close and Freak enjoying a drink at her expense, or KYTVs most likely.

The first thing warms me, Reba thanking me feels good, makes me less of a heel for going by her place, but the second robs me of the warm right away and I get a prickling running over my scalp; I'm afraid of what a woman who makes shows about other people's troubles might do around here.

'Brooke! We're up!' one of her crew shouts at her from the pool table and she makes some comment about seeing them soon as can be, on account of being no good at pool.

'Keep my seat warm,' she tells them. 'There's so much more to talk about, I want to hear all about Porch Lies!'

Lark and Evangeline come hustling up to Beau and I see he gets uncomfortable about the collar and scratches the back of his neck a couple times.

'Beau McCall,' Lark says to him with what I recognise to be her school teacher's voice, 'What do you mean by refusing to let Brooke Adler interview you for her piece about our town? You're the heartbeat!'

'What's this?' I ask and Lark rolls her eyes.

'It's no use telling you,' she says. 'You won't make him change his mind. In fact, if I know you, you probably put him up to it!' She's laughing at me, but if there's anyone left in the world, I don't mind laughing at me it's Lark. Come to that, I'm not bothered one way or another if anybody feels like laughing at me, but what I mean is, Lark, she's just a sweetheart and would rather die than hurt a fellow's feelings.

'I have no idea what you mean,' I say in honesty and she gives me a look like she weren't born yesterday.

'As you know, Brooke Adler is trying to get to know our town. She'd like to feature Beau, because he's one of the oldest residents, but he won't do it.'

Beau mutters something we're not supposed to catch, which sounds a little like he ain't gon help with no 'poverty porn' and chuckles into his beard, which is often his way, and I see a puddle of beer just by his elbow that needs wiping with my cloth before the fringes of his buckskin jacket sleeve does the job for me. I wipe the counter, looking every which way but at Beau, Lark or Evangeline, while they're arguing the toss about the whys and wherefores of being on TV and all the while I'm keeping an eye out always, always along up and over the gathering of bodies, looking for an eye that wants mine or maybe more importantly a pair of eyes that are starting to lose focus, maybe getting a hard glint that tells me I need to delay their next drink or find a way that has them thinking it really is right about time they headed on home before Caleb Armstrong gets what's coming to him or someone tells Mattie Larson something she shouldn't have to hear about how cute her butt is and everyone knows what she's wanting and he's gonna give it to her—tonight's her lucky night. People sure do talk a lot of horse shit, but it's not just working here that reminds me why I don't touch liquor.

Belle has arrived. She comes over and puts her arms around Beau from behind him, gives him a kiss.

'Are they giving you a hard time, old man?' she says and he nuzzles her like he's a fine old dog.

'Nothing I can't handle,' he tells her and swats his hand at the girls. 'They are just a couple of horseflies.'

'Beau!' Lark laughs.

Belle's got her eyes trained above the bar on the TV screen. 'Would you look at that,' she says, voice filled with disbelief.

'What up, Belle?' I ask, fixing her a long glass of seltzer water barely coloured with Jim Beam; Belle likes to say she don't drink.

'That cock-eyed weatherman is calling for snow storms again,' she says, all bent out of shape. 'We did not used to have weather like this around here. If I'd wanted to live in Montana, I'd have moved to Montana.'

Noise comes out of Ev's mouth like a tire fast deflating. 'That your global warming, Belle?' she says.

Belle turns a slow eyed smile on her. 'It's not mine, Evangeline honey.' She sounds like she's talking to one of Lark's 4th Grader's sassing her. 'It's everybody's.'

Now oftentimes Ev will take the bone and work it, and just about anyone knows it's on account of she's up for a little entertainment. Mostly, folks don't take it personal. Tonight though, she's interrupted by Brooke Adler coming over after her game, done so fast it may actually be true that at least somebody playing is surprisingly bad; or maybe they just wanted it over with. Anyhow, here she is making eyes at everybody like she's America's sweetheart.

'So!' she leans up against the bar. 'Lark was telling me you have a monthly story telling jam? How did that come about?'

'Well,' says Belle, settling into her groove, 'would you laugh if I told you it was the closing down of the Giant Walmart that did it?'

Brooke Adler leans in. 'No, I would not, Ms. Belle, because you struck me from day one as a very smart lady, but I'll need you to explain why.'

'Aw, come on,' Ev busts in. 'You've talked about a community story telling since God was a boy, everybody knows that.'

'She's right,' Belle says, smiling; she likes to be known. 'I have always wanted to do something like it, but it was my,' she stops for a beat. 'The Walmart closing was my own personal epiphany. When they finally shut those doors without a thought for the community and what we'd be losing, I knew I had to do something…' She breaks off and says to me, 'what is that smile hiding, young man?'

'I'm just tickled by the way your mind works, Belle.'

'Exactly what is it that tickles you?' she puffs up, but her eyes are full of laughs, so I know I'm okay.

'Well,' I say slowly. 'Most folks thinking about what a community loses when the superstore closes don't fly right away to thinking about storytelling. Most folks are thinking about a 70-mile round trip to the nearest grocery store and who do they know's got a vehicle.'

As soon as I finish saying it I wisht I hadn't; I don't want to get inside Brooke Adler's orbit, but it's too late.

'So, you advocate the do-nothing approach?' she asks, waspy and fast and it ain't just me's surprised by her jumping on me like that.

'I don't think that's what he was saying, were you?' Lark says, turning to me.

I hear the sound of the glass washer clicking done and haul open the steaming rack and start on stacking them above the bar. I say something about it don't matter, I was just passing the time.

'But you've raised an interesting point,' Brooke Adler says, and I know that trick; how to stroke someone to make them cool their jets. She looks around at everybody; so inclusive, you might think. 'And I don't want to overlook anybody's experience when I make this show. It really matters to me that my viewers get a sense of what it really means to live in rural America today.'

I can't think why, but I keep it to myself.

'Something that's been of interest to me for a while now,' she goes on. 'Is the role that passivity plays, within families and communities. Have you ever thought about how huge the impact of doing nothing can be?'

Belle nods. 'Oh yes...' she says. 'Folks *have* to step in. You *can't* be crossing the street, ignoring the man laying in the gutter.'

'Right!' says Brooke Adler. 'People like you understand that, God bless you! So, Walmart packed up and left. Do you sit around and complain? No! You're up and out there, and organising.'

Belle is warming right up now, happy to have a body to expand to. 'What I saw was, we hadn't just lost jobs, we had lost a meeting place. It wasn't ideal, but it was better than nothing. Whenever I did my grocery shop I knew I'd see at least five or six of my neighbours, there was a community board, a coffee shop.'

'Yeah right,' Ev says, bitter. 'But they had to kill Main Street first, it couldn't have become the meeting place if they hadn't done that. I'm just glad they didn't open an auto repair shop too.' She rolls her eyes and laughs at the idea. 'They could have done it in the home improvements aisle, next to the anti-freeze and 3-in-1!'

The mood lightens a little, for them at least and Belle says, 'You know, Evangeline, I try hard to see what I can make, out of any situation life throws at me...'

'Yeah, I know, lemons into lemonade.' She can be as like to one of them lemons as a person can be, Ev, but nobody seems to mind. In fact they seem to get a laugh from it and Lark, on occasion, will refer to her as Oscar the Grouch off of sesame street and say she's gon bring her to Show and Tell at school.

While they're back and forth over that, Brooke Adler leans over to me and touches my arm before handing me a piece of paper.

'Give me a call,' she says low voiced. 'I'd like to ask you a few questions.'

She flashes what I can only assume is meant to be a friendly smile and I smile back feeling anything but. I ball the paper in my hand as she turns back to speak to Belle and I'm tossing it in the garbage, when I catch Beau's eye. He chuckles quietly under his hat, shaking his head a little at the way of the world, no doubt. I step away and continue wiping my way through the last of the steaming glasses.

'What's the next theme going to be?' Brooke is asking. 'I saw on the community website that you always have a theme.'

Belle indicates the two old-timey preserve jars we use for tips and says she'll decide when they're counted at the end of the night. She's wrote on each in her curling, cursive hand. She taps one and says, '*Regret*.' Rolling it out and looking around at everyone, stroking her hands like she's rubbing in lotion. Then she taps the other jar. 'Or, Never Look Back.' She looks at Brooke Adler and says, 'I like folks to decide the theme and it helps give the bar staff a boost to their tips.'

Lark sighs. 'There can't be a living soul who doesn't have a regret of one sort or another. But I hate to look back.'

'You have to look back,' Brooke Adler says as though that decides it. 'If you don't, you just repeat the mistakes from the past.'

'For sure, hon,' Belle tells her and her eyes, heavy with them black lashes she glues on, shine as she says, 'Might be *you* have a story to share, Brooke, honey.'

Brooke Adler laughs, 'I tell other people's stories, Belle, that's *my* calling. I'm happy to leave the stage for others.'

I look at her enjoying centre stage as always when she comes in here and can't help looking at her in disbelief.

I reach for a new cloth and wonder what sort of regrets Lark could have.

'Have you made up your mind which story you're going to share with us, Cassidy?' Belle raises her voice to me.

I sigh and give her an exaggerated eye roll. 'Belle…' I say in a voice I know makes her laugh and I lean under the bar to haul out some more paper napkins.

'She'll get you up there one day, you just wait and see,' Freak laughs.

Somebody calls my name, sharp. I swing over to find Reba standing there sour faced like one of them lemons they're all talking up.

'Hello,' I say. 'Good to see you.' She's scowling at me.

She slaps her pad down, tears off the top sheet and gives me a quick-smart quirk of her eyebrows. Before she can say a word, I reel off the order and give her a nice friendly wink before turning my back on her to start on filling it. Right about then, Brooke Adler leans across the bar and puts her hand on my arm again. I pull away and ask what I can do for her.

'That red-headed woman,' she says, sounding real casual. 'Is she a friend of yours?'

'After a fashion,' I say, keeping busy with my hands.

She laughs and tries again, 'Girlfriend?'

It's my turn to laugh. 'You think she looks like my girlfriend, the way she looks at me?'

'It was more the way she looked at *me*.' Brooke says. 'I don't think she likes that I gave you my number.'

The very idea that Reba would give a hoot about that makes me relax; somehow, Brooke Adler being so far off the mark puts me a little at ease.

'It ain't like that.'

'It's hard to work with your partner,' she says, just like she hasn't heard me.

'That something you know about?' I ask, just for something to say really.

But she takes me at my word and says, real serious, 'My job is too important to mix business with pleasure.'

'Well,' I say. 'I'm sure it is.' And I try and keep the salt from my words and I think I manage it judging from her expression, which looks like she thought I paid her a compliment.

She starts to say something else but I'm distracted by Lorelei Lovett's middle boy, scooching in over by the fire doors, up to no good. I'm torn between letting the kid be and making sure he doesn't get us busted up and shut down —although seeing as we're just about the only place to get a drink around here, I can't see Sheriff Parker actually ever carrying out that threat.

'Billy Lovett,' I say to him as he slides on by, dollar bills in his pocket, bag of weed in his waistband. I beckon him and tell him real quiet, but badass so he takes me serious, 'Next time I catch you in here actin' like this is your own personal command center, I'm a call your mama and see if that don't scare you better than Sheriff Parker.'

Well that does the trick and Billy hightails it out, promising to do his business someplace else. But I'm not liking the way that Brooke, appears to be taking in every little thing going on in here like she's studying for her finals. She flashes me a smile I can't translate, and I turn back to my work.

I'm in the laundromat on the east side of town, wondering if there's anything more soul-sucking than a fully automated washeteria. Ain't nobody to make change, they got a machine for that, ain't nobody to explain the machines, they got a sign for that and ain't nobody to pass the time. Seems to me a fully automated washeteria is a pretty lonely, colour free place.

I transfer my clothes from the washer to the dryer, then reach inside my backpack and start to pull out my small sketchpad. I'm getting to work on a study of a bluebird, when the door swings open, setting off an electronic heads-up that somebody else is about to sit in silence with you.

'I thought that was you sitting there.' I'm like to jump right out of my skin to see that it's Brooke Adler, but I can keep still when I need to, so I just turn towards her and give her a look.

'Did you lose my number, or are you ignoring me?' she asks. There's something a little flirty in her voice, like she can't imagine anybody ignoring her; it's a joke of an idea.

'Ms Adler,' I say and she looks momentarily like I caught *her* off guard. Good. 'It ain't good manners to ignore a person. Are you suggesting I got no manners?'

She colours up. 'What? No. I...'

'Well, what?' I ask, for my own amusement, really; it ain't going to help me none in the long term.

'I think I'd like to buy you a drink,' she says, changing tack. She's good.

'I'm kind a tied up,' I say. 'And I don't see no bar.'

'We can go to my hotel,' she says, and when I look over at my tumbling clothes, adds, 'Surely you're not worried someone will take them?' She's laughing at the very idea.

I guess she ain't never used a laundromat before.

'It ain't worth the risk. They're all I got.'

She stays quiet, standing there looking at me like she's recalculating, trying to work out how to deal with me. What she takes me for I do not know, but I am familiar with the perception some folks can have of me on account of the way I talk.

My mama hated that I talked so country, but half the time I did it just to make her crazy. Like most kids, I suppose, I could talk a couple different ways if I put my mind to it—still can. It depends on who you're talking to and what effect you're aiming for. I know when ain't has no business being in my mouth, but I like how it feels; easy, sliding out without being held up at the pass. Truth be told, I like how it can make folks think I'm not worth the trouble, it keeps them out of my business. If you talk country, folks make a lot of quick-fire assumptions and the first one is always about your intelligence.

'You seem to think I want something from you,' she says. 'Aside, I mean, from the work I'm doing here getting to know you all for my show.'

'Well, don't you?' I say and shove my hands deeper in my pockets. Tap, tap.

'Your name...' her pause comes and goes like a blink and I wonder if I imagine it. 'Cassidy.'

She must've heard how I'm called at least a dozen times, so her rolling it about like that, like she ain't so sure, takes me up a notch. I listen real close.

'You've seen my show,' she says. Not a question.

'I don't have a TV.' She laughs just as I expect her to.

'There's a screen in the bar, Cassidy.'

'It faces the same way I do,' I say, and she laughs again.

Right away she says, 'I may not have spent too much time in this town, but it's plenty enough to see that you can be very friendly when you want to be. So why so hostile?'

I bite my tongue.

'I don't understand. Have I offended you somehow? Or is it really just arrogance, as your friend Lark would have me believe.'

A sharp sting of something I don't at first recognise stops me from speaking. Lark talks to Brooke Adler like that? About me? I feel like I missed a beat somewhere. I feel stupid.

'I'm told you don't *approve*,' she says, mocking. 'Of reality TV. Social media.'

I shrug. 'Is that right?'

'I wasn't always on TV.' She sure does change course quick. 'In fact, there's a part of me that would like to get back to what I used to do.' She stops for a minute, weighing something up, maybe. 'Cassidy, can I level with you?'

Now, generally speaking, when a person says they're wanting to level with you, you can be damn sure, that's when they're going to lie bigger and better than they was already doing. So this just makes me listen even more careful.

'Go ahead.' I smile at her, raise my eyebrow a little. 'Go right ahead.'

She looks as if she's just realised she overplayed her hand; that I ain't quite as dumb as she thinks. 'The dryer has stopped,' she points out. Well, I know that, but I was hoping she'd get out of here before I start parading my undershorts about the place.

'I can help you fold,' she says, and I get up real fast.

'No need.' I haul out my jeans and my shirts, twisted around themselves.

I get myself between her and the door of the dryer, turn my back. I want to sort and fold my clothes without her watching, calculating and before I know it, out of my mouth comes, I'll meet her at her hotel in twenty minutes.

She's gracious and leaves so fast, I can tell she knows I'm already regretting it.

Even so, as I'm hauling ass with my bag of laundry and trying to remember where her hotel is, there's something in me wants to know what she's got, why she keeps circling me. My guess is it's something to do with the video Lark and Ev made me look at and if I can keep her out of Reba's business, whatever it might be, that'd be a good thing.

I see her right away in the dark lobby of the hotel. I ain't never even stood in the parking lot of a place like this, and I feel uncomfortable and kind of dirty, which I honestly am not. She's the only person at the bar aside from two dudes look like they're passing through on business.

Brooke Adler, she beckons me and in an over-loud voice that tells me she already had a couple, orders us both a rum and Coke, which seems kind of early in the day, but hey, who am I? I tell her I don't drink, and she nearly falls off her bar stool.

I'm not certain if this is because she had planned to get me wasted or if she just didn't ever meet a person who didn't drink. Her next question is revealing, it seems to me.

'How long have you been sober?'

I give her a long look before I answer, and she's not satisfied, I can see.

72

'It ain't that. I just never liked the taste of liquor. Lord knows I tried. When you grow up where I did, there ain't much of anything besides liquor and drugs, but I never took to it.'

I wonder if I sound for real to her. My ears are burning anyhow, and I think, you can say a thing all you want, but that don't make it so.

She gets over her shock and begins to talk, and man that woman can talk. I guess it makes sense if you consider the fact that she earns her way by talking non-stop to a camera. She's finished telling me what a wonderful town this is and she's trying to have me believe she's just a small town girl herself, and how she's had this burning ambition all her life to make good and leave all that behind, but lately she's been seeing the merit of small town life and those good, simple people (swear to god that's what she said) and it's all so real, don't you think, Cassidy, and she don't ever want to forget where she comes from and I'm thinking, *Bull. Shit. Bullshit.* If you never saw that old town again and all those real, simple people it would be too soon for you.

Brooke makes short work of her drink and orders another double while telling me about her work. I wonder what kind of a drunk she makes and if I really want to be around to see.

After another few minutes of small-town homage, she starts steering a different direction. She's talking about investigating the fall-out of what she calls human interest stories. You know the kind of thing; I know I do. Other people's tragedies, big time fuck-ups, or just wrong place, wrong time kind of stories, but I'm getting short of breath listening, lightheaded even. Ain't nothing here about Reba or the video and I feel like she's heading someplace I don't want to go, but I ain't got a choice. My heart beats so I notice it as she goes on, and for a crazy minute, I wonder if she can see it, whompin' away in my throat. I wipe my

73

mouth with the back of my hand and look about for a glass of water. I want to get out, but she's still talking.

'What we want to do, Cassidy,' she says my name so often it's sounding a hell of a lot like a code word, but you know, sometimes a drunk will do that; it's a way of showing they're not so fucked up they don't know who they're talking to. 'What we, I, want to do is follow up on socially impactful... impactful stories... that have happened a while ago and catch up with the people involved, see what's happened in the time that's passed.' She orders another rum and Coke. 'I should cut down,' she says, and she actually sounds like she means it, which makes me feel a little sorry for her, for a beat. 'You know... it can get lonely and very... umm...' She halts for a second and I wonder if I should say something, but she focuses again, pretty quick. 'On the road all the time. It's not... People think TV is all glamour and excitement, but there's a lot of nothing while you're waiting around. And there's a lot of travel in my line of journalism.'

'Is that what you call it?' I ask, trying for playful. I'm thinking if I can keep her talking more loosely about her work while she drinks up, then I can get out of here before she suddenly springs something on me.

'You sound like my dad,' she says, and laughs, but I don't think she's amused. 'He thinks it's gutter journalism, that I'm prostituting my talent and education.'

'Well,' I say. 'Might be he's right.'

She don't like that. 'I hold people to account and I'm proud of that. Do you know how many assholes there are out there who think they can do whatever the hell they want, hang the consequences? Deadbeat dads and drunk drivers tearing families apart and just getting a slap on the wrist?'

I was under the impression she just did feel good stories and I tell her so.

'I've been working on the other stuff while doing that,' she says, waving her hand like it's all down the river. 'It's time to use my position for the greater good.'

I snort. I really do. Who was she calling arrogant in the laundromat?

'So you'll make it your business to hunt em down and point your camera at them and let the public be the jury? Shit, lady, you don't think *that's* arrogant? If you think you can get under the skin of a real person and know what all really happened just by pointing your camera at them, you're hell of a...'

She leans close, gets right in my face; enough to make me move back, jumpy. 'It's *arrogant* to pass *judgment* when you don't know shit and all *you* do is work behind a bar.' I'm beginning to see what kind of a drunk she makes.

I try and lighten things up. 'Yeah, I know. But at least I ain't wasting any talent or education to speak of.' But I've misjudged it somehow and she blushes and sounds angry when she replies. 'Now you've made *me* sound arrogant.'

'Sweetheart, you done that all on your own.' I tell her and I lean back and take a long look. Maybe I do want to poke a stick at her, I think, and I wonder what's wrong with me.

'Arrogant *and* patronising. Do you actually hear yourself?'

I shrug. 'It's just the way I talk. I'm not from around here.' The minute I say it, I want to haul it back.

'I know,' she says. 'I know you're not from here and I know when you turned up and in what shape you were in. I know you've run from something. I know that you act like someone who's trying to hide.

'This is a very friendly town, *Cassidy*. And people like to talk. How about you? Would you like to talk? Give me your side of the story? Because you and I both know we're just playing a little game here. You and I both know you're a drunk and a thief, don't we? Some people might even say you're a killer, mightn't they?'

I stand and almost knock the table over. The last thing I see as I turn to leave is a look on her face of irritation and triumph all at once.

There's a heaviness in the air as I make my way through town and on to the barn and even though it's still only around four in the afternoon, the light is going and it feels like the mountains are getting closer, closing in around me. If I hadn't heard the weatherman talking about the aftermath of a hurricane in the Florida Keys, I'd think it was just me. Brooke Adler has put the wind up me, big time.

Back home in my van I lie back and get to thinking. All this last week or so I been wondering how to protect Reba from Brooke Adler and her shitty show, when maybe it's been me she's interested in all along.

I pull out my shoebox and rifle through it, looking for the news pieces I clipped, looking at the names of who covered one story or another, but her name don't come up. Just some fella name of O'Hara and Mountain Herald staff writers.

A few days pass and inside my skin, I'm quietly freaking out. Ain't nothing worse than not knowing what a person's next move is going to be.

At work, I'm takin orders and answering questions about the beer, or listening to Beau or shooting the breeze with them that wants to, but all the time, I'm a mess inside. Oh, I'm putting on a good show, but only because otherwise I'm like to freak out on the outside.

I top a beer for a fella I don't recognise and when I make change for his twenty, he thanks me and says, 'You're Cassidy, right buddy?' I nod and give him a quick smile, which I ain't feeling. He hands me an envelope. 'This is from Brooke. She says you'll know what it is.'

I take it, fold it and shove it in the back pocket of my jeans and try to think of something, anything that ain't what might be in that envelope.

Lark walks in with Evangeline and doesn't seem to see I'm here. It takes me a while to recognise my hurt. In all the time I know her, coming to a year now, she's endeared herself to me on many counts; not least because of taking me as I am. Lately, though, she's taken to asking me questions about before I come here and last night while she was giving me a ride from her parents' farm after a pot-luck supper, she says out of nowhere, 'You should so have kids, Cassidy.'

Well maybe it weren't out of nowhere. I'd taken my mind off of things a little by having a sweet old time, rough housing with her little cousins, playing hacky sack and what have you, so I guess it wouldn't take a rocket scientist to see I like kids. Anyhow, when she blurted that out, I was gladder in that moment that it was she who was doing the driving than you could possibly know; I'd hate to have skidded off the road and lost Mr and Mrs Lund their only daughter.

I stayed quiet with my heartbeat and didn't say nothing for so long that she laughed and said, 'Don't tell me! You left a whole tribe of them back in Mason County or wherever it is you're from!'

Then all the fun went out of her and she shot a look at me. The headlights from an oncoming truck lit her face for a quick time and she looked nervous, unsettled, I guess.

I finally said some words. Something like asking why she would say a thing like that and she talked at me all in a rush, like jumping into a cold mountain lake. 'Brooke Adler knows you, doesn't she?'

I sighed and after a time, feeling weary to my bones, I said, 'She don't know me, Lark. She just thinks she does.'

77

She started to say something, but I cut her off. 'And it don't help me none that you tell her shit that makes me sound like an asshole.'

Well, I surprised the both of us with that. She turned her head sharp to look at me, and the car veered a little before she looked back out on the road ahead.

'What are you talking about?' She sounded mad, but I don't know who at. Brooke Adler? Me? Maybe herself.

'It don't matter, Lark. It's not important.' I wish I had of said nothing. I don't know why I did.

'Of *course*, it's important,' she said, her voice climbing. 'I didn't say anything bad about you. Why would I? What could I possibly say?'

I had nothing to say. Lark drove on in a hot silence, which seemed to me to be waiting for something to break, and when she did finally speak, she didn't tell me nothing I didn't already know.

'You sure know how to hurt a person,' she said; her voice trembled. And right there I heard from her own mouth why always just at the moment where it might be otherwise, when I might lean in, feel warmth, hold and be held, I draw away from her. Lark knows me as I know myself; I know how to hurt a person. Everybody I ever loved got hurt by me, one way or another.

We drove in silence for the rest of the journey and I remember thinking that even with my eyes closed I could tell the rise and dip of the telephone wires, just by the sound they made in the air outside the car and the rhythm of the tyres on the road helped me out as I tried to think of nothing.

When Lark pulled up at the barn, we sat a little while before I moved to get myself out of her car.

'Cassidy?' She didn't sound like her usual self, which weren't no surprise, but it sure made me feel bad. She's been good to me and I hate to see her hurting. 'Ever since

Brooke Adler got here you've been wound up tighter than a spring and it's making me worry.'

'Well, you don't need to be worrying about me, I can take care of myself.' I opened the door of the car.

'Jeez, Cassidy! I know that, for crying out loud. I'm not under any illusions about you. You think that just because I... that I'm so naïve that I can't see things for what they are? Something's happened to you, anybody can see that.' I have to confess that right about then I just wanted her to quit talking at me and drive away. 'Can't you talk about it?' She was looking at me so gentle, her eyes tender, like she cared, really cared about me.

Words started to rise in me, gathered into a hot, hard ball in my throat and I wanted to do it, to tell her. I wanted to tell her about Petey and Harper, about running my mouth off and pride coming before a fall and all that shit, but the words got stuck. I didn't know how to tell her without telling her everything and if I did that, I knew that the look in her eyes would change for good. So I said nothing and stared out across the top of her car until finally she turned the key without looking at me and I stepped back to let her leave.

When I finally get my boots off after work and I'm laying back on my bed, I tear open the envelope that Brooke Adler's left behind the bar and pull out a news clipping and a photograph and have a kind of stupid thought, wishing I'd known there'd be a photo. I wouldn't have folded it if I'd known. It's crumpled and crushed, but it don't matter, I can still see it clear as day. And as I do, it's as though a great flock of birds takes flight inside my head.

I don't bother looking at the guy in the photo, I don't need to, but I look at everything else. I take in the truck parked behind us, alongside Mama's van; Petey's little yellow dumper truck on the deck and the wire dog kennel just aside of it. Finally, I make myself look at the long-haired girl the guy has his arms around, her swollen belly, sticking out tan and proud over the low-hung cut-offs she wore all summer.

Her mama named her Cherish, but she always went by Harper. It was her grandma's family name and did she ever love her grandma, though the way they fought you'd maybe doubt it. I look at the picture and I think how young we were. I notice there's something unsettled in her eyes I maybe didn't pay enough mind to at the time and I look at the man beside her and think, how strange to see myself clean-shaven after so long. I put my hand up to my face, feel the bristle-and-soft of my beard and think that the camera sure can lie. I looked like a fellow without a care in the world.

At last I read the news clipping that come with it, more to make sense of Brooke Adler than a wanting to. I'm scared and my heart don't feel regular in its beat.

'This latest twist has rocked a community already traumatised by a series of tragedies that began with the death of pregnant, 23-year-old Harper Eyman at the hands of her estranged partner. Medics were unable to save the baby. Her grandmother, Lucille H. Godey told The Mountain Herald *that the theft of her grandson's ashes is almost too much for her to bear. 'I don't see how I can go on. What kind of person would steal a baby's ashes? They belong here, with me, beside Harper.'"*

I turn over the photograph and someone has written, Harper and John C, July 2009 and I pass my thumb across the black ink as though I can erase it all.

Every day since Brooke Adler came hustling into my workplace, shaking things up with her TV smile and seeing eye, life has been coming apart. Folks are doing different to their usual and it's making me uneasy. Lark avoids me, Evangeline looks at me strange and resentful and Beau is slow to laugh. All everybody talks about is Brooke's show and if and when she's going to put them in it. Freak and Evangeline are wondering right under my nose why I'm so averse.

'Everybody wants to be on TV,' Evangeline says. 'Unless they have something to hide.'

'Oh, don't be a fool, girl,' Freak answers her. 'Cassidy here doesn't have anything to hide, he's just your regular old introvert, right Cassidy?' He winks at me and then laughing hard at his own joke before it's even out he says, 'So would you be if you had the law on your tail!'

I shake my head slowly at him like I know he's a fool and start to fill a bar order. I almost choke when Ev says, cool as you like, 'Is that why you carry a gun, Cassidy?' She's so deadpan she could be asking about an item of my clothing. 'Law after you?'

I'm not quite sure how she means it, nor how to answer, but I give it a go with the truth, trying to keep my voice as even as I can.

'I ain't never carried a gun and I ain't about to.'

She glances up from her phone screen, eyes to my pocket just as I pat it without realising I'm doing it, then she looks right in my eyes and smiles, hard, before looking back down at the screen in her hands.

'I'm just messing with you,' she says. 'But it doesn't take a rocket scientist to see you've got something worrying you in that pocket.'

She turns to Freak. 'Lark says it's OCD!' and she barks out a laugh. 'She also says you're making things as hard as possible for Brooke; she's never known you so rude and unwelcoming. I wish you'd back-the-fuck off, Cassidy. Some of us could use a bit of excitement around here. And you know, I'm tired of only ever seeing one side of America. I like that she's interested in showing small town people as we are. Decent, hard-working... that we're just as important as all those others living so-called glamorous lives in the cities.'

81

I make the mistake of speaking up. 'You think Brooke Adler is running a PR company for small town America?' I can see her drawing herself up, getting defensive. 'She only wants the dirt. That's all, and if she don't find it, she'll make it up or fall back on caricature and we'll be all over cable TV as the Real Inbreds of Appalachia or something.'

Evangeline starts to say something, halts, then says defiant, 'Well I like her. I think she wants to show us in the best light possible. She grew up in a town like this. She told me so.'

Freak busts out laughing. 'Well that makes it okay, then!'

All while this is going on I'm wishing stupidly that Brooke Adler had never come here with her thrusting ambition and camera crew and strange desire to expose and batter something she claims to love. D'you ever do that? Just wish hard for something not to be, even as you know, you *know*, it cannot be undone?

And through all this, the photograph and memory of Harper keeps pushing and pushing its way into my thoughts no matter how hard I push back. I can't sleep no more without waking after just two or three hours. I'm so tired I can't see right, and a film of white light filters over my eyes every now and again while the skin on my face feels weighted, pulling from my bones.

My camper van is the only place I can breathe, but I can't escape the emptiness that comes on me out of nowhere, then won't leave me be; it's like I'm all hollowed out. And the worst of it, I know this feeling, this dark wash of slow that just keeps on coming. I wish to God I could have left it behind for good. I'm a fool, is what I am.

I've took to walking more, wrapped good against the cold and looking out for any left behind birds that aren't migrated somewhere kinder. I miss the woods and mountains of my home, but this place has its appeal, and I been trying real hard not to look back.

When winter first started slipping from the north this fall, it was Beau who noticed to me that the Canvasback ducks were heading further south than is usual.

'They follow the freeze line on the water, or the freeze line pushes them along, I can't be sure,' he said, amused by his own picture. 'It's been a long time since it's come this far down. Seems to me we have a hard winter coming.' Somehow, now, I keep thinking on that.

Today I take a different route to my usual. Away for once from the fringes, from the woods and water and into town along snow piled sidewalks. It's that time of day when older kids are making their way from school, walking and sliding down the middle of the road, hollering, laughing and rough housing and I find I'm heading the way they're all coming from.

I might catch Lark coming out of school and then I wonder if that's why I came this way in the first place. Like I said, she's been keeping away from the bar ever since I had that ride off of her, four or five days ago and the space she's left behind surprised me before it settled in, unwelcome, unwanted.

My feet slow as I get closer to the elementary school and I watch all the little kids for a while. A couple of the waiting mom's glance over, check me out, before they look over at a fellow about my age with two youngins climbing over him and hanging on his legs. One of the women says something to him and they get talking, comfortable; it's what they all do every day, I guess.

It don't take but a minute before I see what else is going on.

Brooke Adler is facing Lark, just inside the school gates, while her camera crew make sure everything is recorded and filmed. Lark, she's holding hands with two little kids, one a them Reba's little boy and they're all three smiling and answering questions about Horse Neck Creek Elementary.

83

A moment or two passes while I take in the friendly looking scene. Then something changes. An excitable shuffling, a gathering of groups of parents and kids, a parting of the waters and the level of voices rises up.

I hear Reba before I see her, calling out high and sharp and in it, I hear the unmistakeable fear.

'*Sailor!* Get here! *Now!*'

She sure is angry but it's so much more and Sailor, it's like he's been drilled; he knows not to mess with that voice. I see him skedaddle, but he's not fast enough and Brooke Adler follows and is directing her camera man to keep up with her. She's smiling and holding her microphone in his face, asking him something I can't hear but that makes his eyes big and kind of wild-looking, while he tries to see around the camera crew and Brooke and everyone else that's blocking his mama from him. I push my way through the crowd of school kids and parents and regular afternoon passers-by, and I reach them.

'Come on,' I say, huddling my arm around the little boy and scooping him towards Reba. I turn to Brooke in anger, 'What in hell you think you're doing, scaring a little kid like that?' The words come from my mouth on hot steam as I lift up the child and put my hand out to Reba. She don't take it, but she comes right to me and walks fast alongside without taking Sailor from my arms. I can't help but notice how his legs cling around my middle like a little monkey, even while he stretches an arm out to his mama. Reba holds his hand as we hurry along without speaking.

'I'm sorry, mama, I didn't know,' Sailor's saying, real tearful. 'Ms Lund asked if we wanted to tell about school.'

'I know, baby. You're not in trouble. She should have asked me first, though. It's okay, don't cry, now.'

I sneak a quick look at her face and it is a storm barely quelled.

'You okay?' I ask, but she ignores me and as Sailor lets go his grip around my neck and swings away from me towards her, she puts her arms out and takes him. All the while keeping up her fast pace, putting as much space between us and the school as is possible. I look back and see ain't nobody bothering with us now and get to thinking about what kind of a person does that outside a school.

After a time, Reba slows up and takes a breather. Sailor takes a look at me, good and long and I wink at him.

'Okay now, buddy?' I ask him and my heart catches me off guard and tightens in a twist at the pumpkin smile he gives me.

'This is where we turn off,' Reba is saying in her most dismissive tone and I want to say I'll go with them but don't want to be doing to them more of the same. I take a step back before I ask if she's sure she'll be okay getting home. Old Reba comes right back there and then, and raises that sassy eyebrow. 'Cassidy.' Just my name accompanied by a weary exasperation, like I should know better. Which I do. Of course I do.

'Yeah, well. Okay.'

'I appreciate what you did back there,' she says then and that helps me on my way, but as I turn from them and head back towards Levi's and work, I hear the rise and fall of a broken song of a question floating from Sailor's mouth. 'Why did... ask where my daddy... thought he was... you said...'

Reba's sharp voice cuts him silent. I'm left thinking I got as many questions as that little boy, but I ain't a child.

That night I am confronted by the very scene I just lived, played out in front of the entire bar on the TV above my head. It's a long minute before I even notice what is going on, but when Freak starts to whoop and holler, 'We got ourselves a home grown hero!' and folks crowd up and joke with me about not knowing I was such a knight in shining armour I get to feeling real antsy.

85

'Turn it up!' yells someone and there's a cheer when Levi obliges and the local news anchor's voice climbs on up to high volume.

'...chaotic scenes outside a local elementary school this afternoon, when filming for a show on small town success stories was disrupted by one angry parent. Our reporter Brooke Adler is at the scene. Brooke.'

'Yes! Hi, hello, good evening, Helen. I'm here at Horse Neck Creek Elementary School on the south side of this unremarkable but welcoming Kentucky town, where earlier today filming for a new rural reality show was interrupted by...'

At this point I tune out or rather the blood pounding in my ears blocks her voice and I swing the bar up and shoot out to the other side to see an action-packed replay of this afternoon. Everybody in here is chanting and whooping, laughing fit to bust and praising me for 'protecting the lady' and here all I'm thinking is that that is my face, my face, so close to the camera that whether or no I decide to pay Belle a visit and do like Brooke said and get a shave and haircut, my face gon be out there on the local news, recognisable to just about anybody who ever known me.

It's still the quiet part of the evening and I'm leaning against the mirrored counter behind me. The TV, as always, is blaring out over the room and right about now I feel myself get jittery inside on account of it being the time of day that Brooke Adler's show gets trailed, about twenty times in just as many minutes. Tonight, they're following up a report from a couple months ago about state domestic violence programmes and that's just the kind of thing guaranteed to bring me out in a feverish sweat. She's been profiling some place that seems to have all the answers, but nobody wants to fund it.

'...*a public safety crisis, when over half the violent crimes committed in this state alone are committed by the person who says...* "I love you." *Join me, Brooke Adler tonight at 8, when I'll be talking to the founder of the state's largest single-site therapeutic transitional housing programme for victims of domestic violence and I'll be asking Governor Trent some tough questions.*'

Some asshole makes a crack about a good slap never hurting nobody and I wonder if the asshole would like a good slap, just to test his theory. TV cuts to the weather report, telling us we're in for a mix of snow, sleet and something else I miss, on account of Beau speaking up and I turn toward him, 'Have you heard?' Beau is asking me.

'I don't hear nothin'. You know that.'

Beau smiles a little. 'Saying nothing is not the same as hearing nothing...'

I don't ask what he's heard, figuring he'll tell me if he thinks it really matters and sure enough he nods up towards the TV screen and says, 'Your friend over at KYTVs making herself enemies as fast as she's making friends.'

He breaths in full and slow until he's increased in bulk a fair bit, and seems to hold on before blowing out, all the while watching me close with them take-it-all-in eyes of his. I turn away, rub at a spot on the counter.

'Is that so?'

'Well, Belle tells me...' He closes up the box of fixings for his fishing flies and gives me the whole of his attention. 'Brooke Adler promised they'd edit out the little boy and his mama, Reba? But it seems they didn't do that and now she's all bent out of shape.'

'Can you blame her, Beau?' I tell him, not believing a minute Brooke meant to do it.

'Of course not. Little kids don't need to be splashed all over the place.'

Evangeline and Freak have joined us now and Ev says what seems to be on everybody's mind.

'I wonder why Reba had such a shit fit at KYTV like that?' She picks at a bowl of chips that I've just now set in front of them. 'Lark says she's just a regular mom, even if she is a little salty.'

'No such thing,' says Freak, dry as you like, and Evangeline gives a good chuckle.

'True enough,' she says. 'Who all here had a regular mom?'

'Not I,' says Beau. 'My mother smoked a pipe and farmed puppies.'

Ev sets up a wailing, but mostly she's laughing about his mama smoking a pipe and he assures her it was all fine and above board.

'They were happy puppies, honey. She was a fine dog breeder, no doubt about that.'

'How about you, Cassidy? Regular mom?' Ev asks.

'Oh sure,' I say breezy as you like. 'PTA, bake sales, the works.'

Well none of that's true, and I don't for a minute think anybody cares, but it does get me thinking, as I swing around to the other side of the bar and see if there's any folks needing something, that she sure was a fine if not regular mom.

They're still on Reba, or Brooke's pursuit of her story when I scooch back over.

'She's probably on some secret America's Most Wanted list,' Freak says. 'It's always the regular folk, the girl next door, the dude you work with and think nothing of. And it's only ever after the fact that people are observant.' He puts on a high voice and says, 'Well, you know, he had a strange look in his eye, now I think about it.' Everybody laughs, more on account of hearing big ol' hairy Freak talking like a beauty queen than anything else.

Folks are agreeing with him, adding their own nickel's worth, when in comes Lark shoots me as sweet a smile as ever and I'm glad to see it. It sets off a softening inside of me that stays for a short while. 'We friends again?' I ask her, keeping it light.

'Don't be a fool,' she says. 'We were never not friends.' But she looks down a little too late for me to miss her eyes filling. I get a pang of recognition; seems I can't get away from bringing good people to tears. Right inside of me, I feel myself pulling in and away from her.

'Now *Lark*,' Evangeline's voice is getting louder with every swallow of her beer. 'Lark, you have the regularest mom in the whole country, I'll bet.'

'We were just discussing the fascinating Ms Reba and wondering what dirt Brooke Adler has on her,' Freak kindly fills Lark in.

'Can we talk about something else?' she says, sounding as unlike herself as I ever heard.

Evangeline lets out a long low whistle and wags one a them long, engine greased fingers at her friend. 'Testy! Bad day at school, hon? Cassidy, do your job and get this lady a drink, looks like she could use one!'

I raise my eyebrow at Lark in a question, but she don't answer me so I just get on and make her a Sea Breeze and listen to her tell the folks.

'Sailor wasn't in school today and his mom didn't call. Anybody seen her today?'

But nobody answers and Ev's calling out, 'Turn it up! Brooke's on!'

I ignore the request, I got my hands full, but the others huddle and make cheering noises when the credits roll and they're singing along with the theme tune like kids watching Sesame Street.

The bar is filling up, the noise is rising and I'm keeping busy as I like, when Levi comes and asks me if I know where Reba is.

'How should I know?' I hear myself sounding real pissy and he shoots me a look.

'Cool your jets, Cassidy, you seem to take an interest in her is all.' I don't like the mocking in his voice and turn away towards what may or may not have been a shout from a thirsty customer. 'If she does this again, she won't have a job. You can tell her that from me.' He laughs, nasty sounding. 'And Cassidy? Your break is for ten minutes. Ten. Got it?'

I shrug. 'Sure, I know.' I don't know why he's on my ass about that, I hardly ever take my break, but he's been unfriendly ever since he caught me snooping around his office. I can't blame the man.

'Listen up...' Ev waits till she has her everybody's attention. 'It might just be that you're all of you wrong about all this. What I heard was that they're more interested in the guy who they filmed Reba good-deeding to.'

'That's right!' Freak's voice rises up, excited, like he's just remembered something. 'I heard that too, man. It's not *her* Brooke Adler wants, it's that messed up guy crying into his coffee and doughnuts. There's a story there, but Ms. Adler's keeping it to herself.'

Lark murmurs something and starts to sing in a low, sad voice. '*Walk a mile in my shoes, baby, walk a mile in my shoes...*' A song I ain't heard since I was a boy, and I think to myself, there weren't no coffee, nor doughnuts.

'Her camera man says she's like a dog with a bone,' Ev goes on. 'Never seen her like it, he says. She's invited viewers to call in if they know who he is and is extending the time they have to do it in.'

'You guys?' Lark is looking above my head at the screen, moving her closed mouth over to one side then the other, which makes her dimples appear and disappear in a kind of on-off sequence; she always does like that when she's thinking. 'Does anybody else wonder if *Random Acts of Kindness* might... shows like it... might be bad for us?'

'Nope,' Evangeline fires back, without a beat. 'Never wonder about that.'

'What makes you say that, Lark?' I ask, real curious. She loves the show as much as the next guy, maybe more.

She gives me a look I can't quite make out; a mix of shame and apprehension, I guess, which confuses me.

'Look at us,' she says. 'Picking over the bones of someone else's pain.'

Ev snorts, but Freak, he laughs.

'Awww, Teech,' he says, putting on a whiny kid voice and they all laugh, even Lark. 'You want us to stop rubber-necking?' He shifts about in his chair, drains his glass and pushes it my way raising his eyebrows. 'What do you say, Cassidy? You think she's right?'

I don't say nothing, just give him his next drink and look at Lark, hoping she'll go on, but knowing that no doubt, Ev will keep the stage.

'What brought this on, Lark?' Beau asks and he leans back on his stool. She looks at him with a smile.

'I don't know. I mean, I love Brooke Adler. This show right now?' She waves her hand up towards the TV. 'This is a really important public service, right? People should know how common domestic violence is, that it could be your neighbour, that we shouldn't turn a blind eye, but *Random Acts of Kindness*? Maybe it's lost its way, maybe we're spending too much of our energy looking at the wrong things, rewarding people for things that don't need rewarding…'

This is way too much for Evangeline, who busts in, 'You think they should be punished?' She laughs at her own joke.

'Mmm…' I hear Beau winding himself up for action. 'Because of course that's the only alternative.' He turns to Lark. 'What's on your mind, honey?' he asks her, but Ev's on a roll.

'You don't like folks *interfering* in other folks' business?' she laughs like she's real clever. 'And here was I, all this time thinking you were a community minded kind of gal!'

Lark shrinks a little, moves closer to Beau, but she's looking at Ev. 'I've been thinking about having to have your good deed recognised. Are we getting to a place where people won't do a thing unless they get some kind of reward?'

She looks a little bashful and I'm just about to tell her to go on, when Ev busts in. 'What's wrong with being rewarded for doing the right thing? You do a thing, you get something back, you feel good, you're more likely to do it again! Win-win!'

'Oh I don't know...' Lark is backing off in the heat of Ev's confidence and it stirs something in me.

'Sure, you do, Lark,' I tell her and she give me one a them smiles again that make me feel good. 'Tell us what you been thinking.'

'Oh it's nothing. Just, I was listening to this show on the radio about the Crash and about the bankers and everything—it didn't make a whole lot of sense to me, but something really hit me. And it got me thinking about my fourth-grade kids...'

'Lark! Get to the *point!*' Ev loves to laugh at her.

'I am, Ev. Stop butting in! The guy on the show was saying that more and more, kids grow up only doing right or whatever, because of what they'll get in return—you know, like star charts and rewards and paying them for household chores...'

'Give me a break, Lark, you want child slave labour in the home, now?' Ev still ain't looked up from her screen, but for a second at a time.

I see Lark flush and her words are coming less confident. 'Well of course not, but... there... he, this guy was saying that we're training a generation of people who'll only respond to bribery and that's how you end up with huge bonuses, which are unsustainable and...' she trails off at Evangeline laughing and shaking her head.

'Sounds like one of those freakin' anti-capitalists—what radio station *was* this, Lark?'

I want Lark to say more, but all I do is fill up the water jugs waiting on a tray beside me and mop up the spills.

I keep real still, and quiet my insides. Lark watches me for a moment. I look away first.

All at once the level of talk and noise drop at the same time, for no reason. It happens all the time without you ever really notice it, but this time it happens just at the moment Brooke Adler's voice coming from right above my head says, '*And it's when they leave that they are actually in more danger than at any other time during the relationship.*'

There was a time not so long ago I really did feel like a boy without a care and maybe even in that photograph of me and Harper and that unborn child I still was. A little bit. But it comes as no surprise to me that now when I'm walking alone, when I'm feeling the space and air around me, catching the always surprising red of a Cardinal against the icy branches of the naked trees, it comes as no surprise in my mind I can see all them doubts and fears that hovered, taking flight around us like they was actual birds themselves. Well, leastways that's how it looks to me now.

We used to sit on the porch, she and me, telling each other baby names and what all we'd do with him when he arrived. But only one name would do for her.

'I want you to give him your name,' she'd say and hook a finger around a piece of my hair, right at my neck. I can still feel the warm of her hand on my skin there sometimes, before I shake it off for stupid.

'Well, that's fine. I'd like that.' And I did, too, but somehow it fed my wondering when she said it; the wondering if it *was* my child and the if it mattered. And just as if she knew what I was thinking, she'd say more.

'Your first name too, so he's all you and you all him.'

93

Well, I weren't so sure of that and told her so, but she said it was a good, honest name and that made me smile.

Now, walking out in the woods in the prickling sharp air left over from last night's ice storm, I find myself wondering how it was I believed we were going to be making our own family together. How in all honesty it was that I could have missed that hum of fear; of maybe he'd come after her. We were kidding ourselves like only youngins in love can do, I guess, and I loved that girl more than I could just about stand.

I'm distracted by the street door swinging open and a rowdy crowd of folks about my age looking to increase their fun by any means, comes elbowing through to where I'm at behind the bar. It don't take me but a minute to sort them in my head: big grizzle-haired fella with a roll to his gait calling the shots; pale looking guy who checks him out before he hazards a word, laughing at every damn thing comes out of that Big Grizzly's mouth and he ain't even that funny; they never are. Then a couple of others along for the ride looking like just about any entertainment would do for them right now and that ain't a way of saying they're easy going.

In a job like this, after a while you get to feeling as though there's always going to be someone wants to make trouble and it's a wearying thing. Don't get me wrong; I get why folks want to act out—some of them, that's all they got. I always hoped I'd someday outrun the kind of places where it was in my face all the time, is all. Yeah, I know, I don't lately come off as the hopeful type, but I have it in me.

I throw a glance Levi's way and he nods. He's background noise, Levi, but the longer I work here the more I realise nothing seems to slide by his notice.

'What can I do for y'all?' I say, taking a breath and readying myself.

'Well, now!' says Big Grizzly, leaning an elbow on the bar to hold his self up. 'You can settle an argument for us.'

My heart sinks, it truly does. That has got to be one of the all-time worst things a barkeep is asked to do, especially if them that's asking's already got glazed eyes.

I make sure I smile and keep moving. Wiping the counter, racking up glasses, spotting the room for anything needs my attention. I keep my eyes off of his and say, light as I can, 'I'll do my best, but I ain't nothing but a barkeep, so I may disappoint.'

'Well, my buddy here says he's seen you somewhere before—isn't that right, Harlan?' he throws a look at the pale fellow, who nods real vigorous. 'He wastes a lot of time watching all the shows—you know the kind of thing, *America's Most Wanted*, Brooke Adler's *Random Acts of Kindness*—fool thinks he's going to make a name for himself by locating one of them and calling it in!' he gives me a phony conspiratorial look like his buddy Harlan is a clown, but in truth it's me he thinks he's fooling. 'Seems to me, he sees them everywhere. Now Harlan here is convinced you are the mystery cry-baby Brooke Adler is hunting up, off of The Waffle House Waitress video.'

We laugh, but the blood is rushing in my ears; these fools and their TV shows. I look at him straight and smile a little wry, like he and me understand each other.

'Well, sorry to disappoint.' I raise my hands.

'You got a name, bud?'

I laugh. 'I sure do,' I say and get back to scanning the room and taking orders.

There's a hard look in his eye before, to my surprise, he lets it go and swats at Harlan with his hand and his voice. It don't make me any more relaxed, though. There's something too calculating about him for that. I'm distracted by my name called.

I didn't even see Lark come in. I wonder how long she's been standing there at the bar. I feel twisted and tight, the easy way between us gone, and wonder if she feels it too. 'You want a ride home after work? It's fixing to storm.'

I throw a glance at Grizzly who seems to have forgotten me for the moment. 'You don't want to hang around till so late, Lark. Don't you have to teach school tomorrow?'

She smiles a little and says, 'A man who doesn't know when it's the weekend, is a man who needs to take stock.'

'Ah… well, still. I finish kind of late.'

Her chin comes up and her eyes water, then she blinks and says, sharpish, 'I know when you fin… oh, forget it.'

I can't make out the look she has. It's sort of shame, but anger too and hell, I know them two often hang together, but I can't see what she has to feel that way about. All the same, I tell her if she finds herself still about the place when I'm done, I'd be glad of the ride. I only say it on account of her wanting me to, though; truth be told, I'd sooner be alone.

By the time I'm finished up at work, Lark is gone, and the place still and quiet. I call goodnight to Levi, who don't never seem to go home, and head out into the street. I'm thinking about what the big guy said in the bar tonight and it give me a curling shame. But there's a burn of fire in me too, right in my chest, wanting to bust out and scorch everything about me. I'm always swallowing and swallowing and I don't know for how much longer I can do that.

I bend my head into the wind and set one foot in front of the other, focusing on a rhythm of sorts and try to hear the sound of my feet on the salt-gritted ground instead of all my thoughts; the questions I pose and answers I try to find. I remind myself that once I get into it, get my blood up, I'll feel okay, but it's taking longer'n usual and I stop for a moment at the edge of town. What in hell am I supposed to do? I make myself breathe, look up at the shaved edge of moon and think that it'll look the same, wherever I am. Lark comes to mind and Beau, sitting at the bar night after night and I feel sadder than I thought possible, wondering if it's time to move on again.

I'm rounding the curve of road that brings me to the creek in back of Beau's, just about managing not to fall on my ass as I feel my feet slide out from under me; gritters hadn't made it out here and rarely do, but I'm not mindful as I usually am. I make myself take a moment, despite the freeze and it's then I notice the barn door open. Not all the way, but enough so's I know it ain't how I left it.

I walk silent as I know how, across the bit of field towards it, my heart pumping hard enough to get in the way of me hearing good. Shit. I stop again, breath deep and press on. It seems to me that every frozen blade of grass, every dried-up twig is cracking loud enough to wake the dead and whoever is in my barn is just listening to my approach. I make myself slow right down, pausing between each step until I get right up to the barn door. And now I'm cussing myself for not changing that damn lightbulb, because the likelihood, I tell myself, is that the wind just got in about the place, or Beau was in there after something and didn't close it right. If I could just throw on the light and see myself, I'd feel a whole lot better.

I feel around the wall inside the doorway for something that might stand in for my missing nerve and put my hand on a hooked pole Beau uses to pull down the ladder to the hayloft. It's real still and quiet inside and I hold my breath, trying to catch a sound shouldn't be there. Nothing.

The stretch from the door to my van is longer than I ever knew it and time pulls itself out between me and it. I promise myself I'll never go nowhere again without a flashlight and finally get to my van. Door's shut. Nothing for it but to open it up and get in there. My hand on the knob, I wait then pull it open hard.

'*Who's here?*' I shout, but it's silent, save for my hard breathing.

I stand in the doorway for a time, listening, looking around and it's so small I can see right away, ain't nobody in there, before I even get the lamp lit. It runs dim, telling me I need to charge it soon and I think, well, everything looks as I left it. But I can't shake off the unease and a certainty that someone's been here.

It don't take but a moment before I see the disturbance under the bench. It ain't much, the rug that works as my comforter is caught up in some of the vinyl, but it's enough and I drop onto my knees, reach under to find my shoebox. I open the lid and my skin seizes, like it's shrinking at speed over my scalp, then tingles back to life, giving me a sweat.

News clippings are stuffed in, crumpled, one a them torn along the edge, and the hospital bracelets have rose to the top, come out from where they been buried this past year and a half. I pick up the first one, hold it in my hand, rub my thumb along its smooth insides. How can this be all that's left?

All that long summer, after Harper left her home and came to be with me and Mama and Petey, my doubts took shape outside of me and floated through the heat-shimmer or came at me like the moths when the sun set.

And it took me a little while to notice the sliding looks and halts in conversation when we walked together through the jiffy mart or joined a group coming out of church into the sunlight. I'd tell myself it didn't matter none, any fool can get a girl pregnant, that don't make him a daddy, it's what he does beyond and for good that gives him a right to that name and, I told myself, she wanted what I wanted so it didn't matter, truly. As long as she wanted me, none of that other shit mattered.

But it seems to me that other folks did have a problem with who the baby's Daddy was. It became the focus of talk around us and anybody tells you talk don't hurt, ain't never themselves been the topic; it hurts like the slow leak of battery acid till you can't recognise what was.

Most times they hid what they thought or shut their mouths at least, but one or two felt it their business to tell me I was either a saint or a fool.

'Why do you let folks talk to you like that?' she asked me one day.

'Like what?' I knew what she meant.

It was a real hot day and we was minding Petey and his buddies down at the creek in the gorge behind Mama's. She was forever telling Harper how lucky she was to have her around and mind him for her, on account of the summer vacation being so long and her never getting time off from the drugstore to take care of him.

'I don't know what all I'd do if I didn't have you around, hon,' she'd say. And Harper'd smile like sunshine and say right back, 'Oh, I love to do it, Summer, Petey's a sweetheart.'

And not a one of us would say a word about why she was with us, living with me and my little half-brother and my mama, when her own grandma still lived over the hill.

'I mean it.' Harper, she would get on one sometimes and not be able to leave it be. 'Why do you just sit back and say nothing when people talk ugly like that? Telling you you're just the clean-up man? A man's protective of his girl, calls out anyone disrespecting her. A man won't let people push him around.'

I said something about I'd never minded other people and neither should she and took myself down to the edge of the water, hollering at the boys again not to stand up in the raft. But I was thinking about what had been said.

She and me, we played together as kids. Roamed all over on our bikes or on the rough-coated pony she'd had from forever, until mama got me a yellow and black dirt-bike off of a dude at work who owed her some money.

All through elementary school, Harper was my good friend and I hers. Her grandma, Lucille, was close friends with my mama and we always bunked together when they got too drunk to drive across the mountain roads back home. I remember hot nights on a big old mattress pulled out onto the screened porch, me and Harper laying together whispering and listening to Lucille and Mama as they sat on the steps, drinking and talking, smoking the cigarettes they always said they was going to quit tomorrow; next week; before too long. We'd try and make sense of what all they were saying, but our own whisperings and stories would take over. I'd never know I'd fallen asleep until the sound of the birds was waking me and the air had the soft hush of early and Mama and Lucille would be curled up alongside of us, sleeping off the night.

One time I told her I was going to marry her some day and she said, 'I know,' just like that and then shushed me so we could listen to Mama talking about my daddy.

'He sure was something else, that one,' she'd tell Lucille and something would pass between them, a look or word we didn't get, so Lucille would make a noise in her throat to make them both hoot with laughter.

'Hoo whee, girl!' Lucille would say. 'I sure could use some of that!'

We both of us wanted to hear all about him, on account of his playing harmonica in a bluegrass outfit that toured all over, and Mama never talked about him unless she was drinking with Lucille. But I never told Harper that I hated to hear it too. I couldn't explain, so I said nothing. She seemed to know it was a sore spot, though, and got a ton of mileage out of that, whenever it suited her.

'You know what?' she hollered at me one day when I'd riled her up about something—she had a temper on her from time. 'I don't think you ever did have a daddy like that anyhow! You're just a lame-assed goober-head, no wonder he up and left, once he seen your sorry-ass face!'

But she was always sorry after and I could never stand to see her all red faced and crying for long, without I'd forgive her. I was her only true friend, she said, and she couldn't be without me and I knew this to be so. It was the same for me.

There weren't nothing out of the way in having no daddy about the place. Families where I come from shape up in all kinds of ways. Harper had a mama somewhere, but nobody knew where; she was a real youngin, just in high school when she had her baby, named her Cherish, then lit out with a flat-bed truck driver from Arkansas, leaving the baby with her own mama. That was Lucille.

Then everything changed when we got to middle school. It took me a while to see it. I never did care that my buddies ribbed us something terrible for being so close; they wasn't rough about it and liked to hang with us in the gorge. But then Grady arrived.

His daddy had got laid off from a foreman's job at a coalmine on the other side of the county and it was as though Grady his own self had been laid off. And right away he made it his business to show who was boss.

Brooke Adler comes into the bar and I realise she ain't been about for a while. My stomach knots tight. Her once again arrival, sets up an atmosphere that winds its way through the entire bar until all ev'body's doing is running their mouths about her show, and all in all giving me just about the worst headache I ever had.

It's not just the way she comes in here like a homecoming queen, flashing that smile and buying drinks all round, which sets my teeth on edge. It's that all them that's drinking up, courtesy of KYTVs surprisingly generous budget, all them people just seem to take her at face value. What's wrong with everybody? When did folks forget she has a show to make and an agenda to fill? Only Beau declines to let her pay for his glass of Wild Turkey, shaking his head in her direction and frowning a little.

'She never heard of Hugh O'Connor, I guess,' he says with a sad shake of his head. Well either did I, but I don't get a chance to ask him on account of you-know-who her very own self, angling her way over to me.

'Hello, stranger.' Voice raised above the noise of talk and laughter and TV, Brooke leans in and taps my hand where it rests on the bar and I actually feel myself flinch before I can check myself. She notices, I can see she does, and for a moment there's something in her eyes a little different to that sharp, seeing look I've come to expect. It can't be regret, people like her don't regret, so I ignore it.

'Well, now,' I say. 'It ain't me's the stranger.' She looks at me, irritated and opens her mouth to say something, but I get in first. 'What can I get for you?' I break eye contact with her, but I keep my voice light and friendly. I get on with tapping a keg while I wait for her to answer, hefting it into place underneath the bar and enjoying her being momentarily on the back foot. Well what did she think? I'm going to play her flirty game while she tries to dismantle my life as I know it? She sure don't like it if you change her script, though and she'll take a while to thaw. No doubt about that.

'My usual,' she says and I just keep looking at her like I don't remember what she drinks. Small thing, but it works. 'Rum and Coke,' she says a little uncomfortable. I start to fix her drink. Evangeline is standing right close to her and starts complimenting her and teasing, in that way some girls seem so easy with.

'Brooke, you have the prettiest figure,' she tells her, looking her up and down, face admiring. 'I only wish I could put calories away like you do without it showing up next day when I can't fasten my jeans.'

Brooke Adler looks pleased, but not surprised, and I tune out as they carry on with carbs and calories and waistlines. Lark looks over at me and raises her eyebrows kind of funny and I smile back. She checks out the two women, then says a little over-loud, 'I think Ev's angling for more than a walk on part in Brooke's reality show, if it ever gets made!'

Everyone laughs, but Ev looks a little put out and Lark gives her a hug. 'You know I love ya, Ev!'

'Brooke tells me,' Evangeline has her on a real dignified sounding voice and it makes Lark laugh right out loud, as was meant. 'I'll just *have* to be a Featured Focus, like it or not, because it's not everywhere you have a lady mechanic who runs her own business. It'll subvert the stereotype, she says.'

I throw a look at Brooke Adler who looks real pleased with herself and give me a face that says, see?

'Well, I guess that may be true,' I say, noticing that I'm running low on pretzels and wondering if Levi's about. 'Small mercies and all that,' I mutter. Ev and Lark head off to the pool table after someone shouts they're up and I'm left with Brooke Adler.

'Cassidy,' she says, and my heart starts right away to bang. 'Have you given any more thought to my request for your story?'

I quit wrestling with the empty pretzel box and look at her. Somehow, I want to laugh and she seems to see that; she squares up to me a little.

'What "request"?' I know I don't help myself by my tone, but that don't seem to stop me. 'I don't recall no *request*.'

'I left an envelope for you with a request...'

Inside I'm beginning to churn up real rough, but I try my damnedest to keep it all still on the outside. 'Why'nt you call it what it was, lady. That was a threat and you know it.'

'Oh, for goodness...' she begins, with that dismissive patronising voice I heard in her once or twice before, but I'm in.

'If you was a decent person, you'd respect a person's right to privacy.'

'If you were a decent person,' she snaps back, 'you'd stand your ground and face the consequences, instead of running away. I follow the story. It's my job.'

'Follow? Ain't what you do twisting? Twisting so it fits your story? The one you already decided on?'

I don't know why I'm doing this; I know it's pointless; she wants what she wants.

'Do you really not care what people think of you?' she asks me then.

I sigh. 'Not a whole lot.' But even as I say it, I know it for a lie; if I didn't care, I'd still be there, wouldn't I?

'I don't understand that.' She pauses and takes a big swallow of her drink, meets my eyes with a hard challenge and goes on. 'Most people, given the opportunity, would want to put their side of the story. Get it out there.' She shoots me a sly old look.

'I ain't most people.'

'So you seem to think. One rule for you another for everyone else, isn't that so? Do you have any idea of how... You do know what people say about you in Mason County, don't you? The stories they tell?' Even though I been expecting this, it still punches me right in the gut hear her mention home out loud like that. She waits for me to say something and when I don't, goes on, 'I *know* who you are; it's not a hunch anymore. I know. I've been there. I've talked to people who knew you. They've told me the whole story.'

In that moment all I feel is contempt; for her; for them. There is no way, no way anybody could of told her anything close to the whole story, but all I say is, 'Well then. You don't need me, do you?' I start to swing away from her and check out who all does need me; bar's filling with locals and out of towners passing through and I crank the sound of the juke box a little. 'Seems you can make out okay without my help.'

Brooke has followed me along the bar and a couple folks leaning up waiting for my attention take umbrage with her sliding along, nudging them out of the way before she leans across the bar and says in a low voice, filled to the brim with disgust, 'I don't know how you can live with yourself.'

I look at her through a haze, fighting down the rising up in me of pain and anger at being judged and cursed all over again; as though I'm not doing a fine enough job of it my own self, every God-forsaken day.

'You know what?' my voice is cracked and dry. 'I can't. I can't live with myself.'

I step right back and take a deep suck of air, but it just makes me feel dizzy.

'Well,' she says, for the world as though she's won something through hard work. 'At least you've got a conscience.'

I mean to put down the tray of empty bottles, but when I hear the smash of glass, I look down and see I've dropped them. The sound seems huge, folks clap, someone whoops, but I stand frozen.

Next thing I know I got Levi on my back.

'Take a break, Cassidy. Take fifteen.' He looks mean red, is what he looks. 'Come see me after your shift.'

He's over by Brooke Adler now and I don't know what all he's saying to her or she to him for that matter, but she's making open palm peace gestures with her hands and shaking her head and smiling regretful, but it looks so phony and I wonder at Levi buying it. Me though, I feel full of shame and anger and can't believe I let her get to me.

Lark is by my side asking if I'm okay and looking suspiciously at Brooke Adler, but I can't speak. I notice the spot where her hand was warm on my arm, as she lifts it, and heads towards Levi and Brooke.

Out in the cold dark by the dumpsters, smoking a cigarette, I think to myself that most likely, there's Brooke Adler thinking that my true nature has finally showed itself and I'm wondering, maybe that *is* my true nature. Maybe just because you don't act a certain way most of the time, maybe that don't necessarily mean it ain't your true nature. Maybe your true nature comes out only sometimes, when conditions are right. And who truly knows anybody? You might think you do, but really, you don't. There's always something gon surprise you. Sometimes I barely know my own self. Sure, I tell myself a story all the time about who I am, but who tells even themselves the whole truth?

The side door opens, letting out a whomp of noise; voices, shouts; the bang and ring of the pinball machine and a whole bunch of cussing, before it slams shut and everything goes muffled again. It's cold and as I blow out the smoke from my cigarette, I play a game of seeing when is it the tobacco smoke and when is it my own breath clouding out. I realise I'm way longer than the fifteen minutes Levi gave me and turn to go back in and nearly jump right out of my skin. It's Lark, but not looking any way I ever seen her.

She's standing a little way off in the shadows, staring at me like she don't know who I am.

'Hey,' I say, guilty for the weariness that pulls through me at the sight of her.

It seems like more and more, every time I see her, it's going to be hard work and I'm more tired than I can remember. Tired of no sleep, tired of hiding my true thoughts, tired of worrying, tired of constant fucking people asking fucking questions, thinking they know the answers. But mostly? Mostly I'm just tired to death of myself.

Lark says nothing, which makes me even more uneasy with myself. She just keeps on standing there, looking at me, but not really at me. Then I realise that she's breathing strange, like she's struggling with it and it makes me feel choked up for a short minute.

'Lark?' I say, hoping she can hear my heart. 'You okay?'

She cries and I reach to put an arm around her, but she moves away. I try not to show my hurt and ask her again what all is wrong. She looks at me at last and that sweet face of hers is streaked and swolled up and she's got tears that keep spilling and spilling. I don't try and touch her again, not with my hands, but I try again to say something and hope that maybe works.

She's looking at me so strange, my belly feels like it's got tiny wires short-circuiting inside. All I can think is, surely there weren't enough time. I only been out here twenty minutes or so.

'What, Lark? She said something to you. What is it?'

When she speaks, her words are lost in her sobs and it takes me a little while to make sense of them. When they do, I freeze inside and lose all the words I ever had. 'I want you to tell me it's not true,' Lark is saying. 'I want you to tell me it's *not true*.'

I think I might pass out. I truly do, so I sit on a step and lean forward.

'It isn't true, is it? What Brooke just told me?' I guess she didn't need much time.

'I don't know what all she told you, Lark.' My voice sounds strange to me, kind of strangled, I feel choked.

'I think you do.' She sobs on them last words. 'What do you think she *could* have told me, Cassidy? There is

107

something isn't there, otherwise you wouldn't... why would you have... You don't even use your real name!'

'It's complicated,' I say. 'But maybe not so bad as you think.'

'Well it sounds pretty bad to me.' Her voice rises shrill and scared sounding. 'She says your name isn't Cassidy at all, that your name is John McArthur and you...' She breaks into sobs again and I wonder how she's going to say it and how many it'll be. 'She says you killed two people.'

My mind, for a time, is hollow. At last I say something.

'I got blood on my hands.' It comes out in an old man's voice and I am so weary I can't say any more, can't explain. I never could find the words; I'm a fool if I think I might find them now.

I look up again and see she's still there. Lark. 'If that's what Brooke means,' I tell her. 'I can't deny it. I got blood on my hands.'

She says my name as all the air comes out of her. 'Oh, Cassidy...' she says, as though everything in the whole world has changed, then moves in my direction and I jump up real fast which seems to frighten her. I feel my heart slip a little as I step back.

'You don't need to be scared of me, Lark,' I tell her and she stiffens.

'I'm not... I'm not scared, I'm just...'

But I know a lie when I hear one, even if it's hid; don't matter that she maybe wishes it was the truth.

The door bangs open and we look around towards it, she like a whip, me in slow drive and Levi's voice come out of the big shape of him in the doorway.

'Okay, Cassidy,' he says. 'Back to work, I don't pay you to socialise.'

For a minute, it's impossible for me to move. My feet are like roots right down through the concrete of the parking lot and I know I'm looking at him like I'm a fool with no

108

understanding of words. I don't want to leave Lark like this, but I can't talk right now. I need to get my head straight. It's hurting so bad I can't think what to do.

'*Cassidy!*' Levi's sharp now, but before I can move, Lark says to me, 'It's okay.'

There's something understanding in the sound, of what I can't be sure, but something of her old self is in there somewhere and I want to reach out and take a hold of it; hang right on.

Levi, unwilling maybe to trust I'll come in without he stands there and watches me do it, continues to bulk up the doorway.

'W… what time is it?' I hear myself stammer—long time since I done that—and I look at my wrist for a watch ain't been there in years. I feel a wave of sickness come over me. Okay, I whisper in my head, move it, John C.

I make myself, make myself turn away from Lark, walk on past Levi and into the noise and dark, through the bar, till I'm standing in my usual place, everything familiar but far, out of reach so to speak. There's a ringing in my ears and for a moment or two I feel as though I am outside of myself, looking on, watching. But then I see Brooke Adler sitting with my friends, talking, drinking with them and a great lunge of something ugly comes heaving from the pit of my belly. I can barely see. I swallow hard and without thinking, swing around and head for the back door, bumping against the edges of fixtures, the sound of voices raised at me for knocking their drinks. It don't cross my mind that I might lose my job.

Outside, I stop for a moment and I get a prickling across my scalp; I'm sure somebody's about but I see no one, just shadows leaping out then sneaking back into hiding. Wind's blowing the branches about something crazy and way high up, there's a bunch of clouds moving fast across the sky.

Without knowing where I'm headed I walk, breathing deep, trying to stop this brawling in my head from busting it apart. If I can think clear, I might be able to work out what to do. Maybe I should talk to Brooke Adler, get things straight; part of me is so tired of running, of hiding, it feels like an idea, but then I remember how these things go. You say a thing in good faith, but then you blink and it's got twisted and bent out of shape and them's your words still, and you can't dispute em, but somehow all your own meaning's gone. Maybe if I just sit tight, let the storm pass and see what's left. But I know how that goes too; stares, nods, silence then one day you find you're all alone without a smile or a friendly word ever comes your way anymore.

I keep walking hard, but I can't think straight nor clear and I have a nasty feeling of being followed. Shit, I ain't been this paranoid for time and it gives me a deep fear that I'm going down and nobody to catch me. I put my hand in my pocket, feel for my box and tap it, one-two. I remind myself I'm the only crazy who walks everywhere, ain't nobody else going to be out here. I throw my head back and start to jog. Maybe if I get my blood pumping it'll help.

I pull up, breathless, nose stinging from the cold air. It sure is a beautiful night. Silent and misted with frozen air. All I can hear is my hard breathing and the pump of blood in my ears. I take in my surroundings; get my bearings and my heart slides down the chute. What in hell is wrong with me? How is it I ended up here?

I'm standing outside of Reba's home and shame runs up and over me. I can't leave her be and that troubles me. But before I can turn and leave, I just about leap out of my body and die right there and then, as somebody grabs me from behind, twisting my arm round behind me, so hard I think it might break and I can't help but holler. A big ol' hand clamps over my mouth so hard my teeth bite right into my lip. I taste my own blood, salty. I can smell liquor and leather and weed and manage a breath before my head

110

gets hauled back so hard I can barely swallow. For one real minute I think he might snap my neck and I panic, struggle, try and bite the hand, but he grunts and tightens his hold, kicks me hard in the back of my knees so they give way. He holds me up and puts his mouth against my ear. His breath is hot and wet, sour-heavy with smoke.

'Be. Still, you *fuck*,' he whispers in my ear and man that is more scary than someone hollering at you, I can tell you. I go quiet as I can and try and still my thoughts. I wonder if this is it; the end for me, and my heart won't lay down and I'm afraid he's going to hear it, tear it out. I'm all fear and shame and rage.

'Now tell me something,' he goes on, still in that fearful creeping whisper. 'What the fuck are you doing sniffing around her house like this, day and night like some pervert?'

This gives me a deep and heavy chill. Does Reba know he's here watching her house, keeping prowlers away? This makes me shamed again when I think maybe she's asked for him to keep an eye out on account of me, her weird co-worker. That's not who I am, but I can't speak up for myself on account of his hand still being clamped hard over my mouth and I'm freaking out inside 'cause I can't breathe and I don't know if he's carrying a weapon and he's about to stick me with it. And anyhow, what would I say? I don't know why, but I want to be near her. That *is* creepy; say it like that.

At last he lets me go, but I don't get a chance to take a look at him; he gives me a couple left-rights so hard, inside of my head bursts white lightning and I fall where I'm standing, my knees hitting the ground hard. I feel the shooting pain of his foot kicking me in my belly, back, belly again, then right in the balls for good measure and I nearly throw up right there. Next thing I know, that voice is rasping in my ear again.

'Stay away. You hear me? Stay away or I'll fuck you up so bad you won't be able to say goodbye to your mama'n daddy. You hear me?'

It's forever before I can open my eyes. Maybe it's no time. I don't know. Round and round my head, one thought runs: get up... get up... get up... My body won't comply. I feel like I'm floating, I'm leaving, I think. Good. Got to get my ass out of here before he comes back.

'You have to get up. Can you get up? Cassidy, get up. Get up.'

I open my eyes; close them again. That was someone else, that wasn't me. Who...

'Cassidy, I can't lift you, you're too big; you have to get up. Come *on*...' impatient, tearful.

Okay, I say. But it's only in my head.

'For Christ's sake you'll freeze if you don't get up, come on. I'll help you, but you have to try.'

Okay, I say, trying harder, but it's still in my head and now I'm feeling impatient. Leave me alone. Through my haze, the pain the float and fog, I hear a whimper.

'Oh god...'

'Okay...' I sound strange, my words swollen, stopping just before they make their exit.

'Good, okay!' Brighter, sharp. 'Come on.'

Well whoever you are, you're better'n the last person had their hands on me, so I do like I'm told and pull myself up. My body screams, throbs and I think I'm gon be sick.

'Slowly, it's okay.'

Arms slip underneath mine and lift as I heave myself up again. Curls fall and sweep against my cheek, then disappear. Reba. I want to cry.

Inside, it's dark. A little warmer than outside but chilly and I wonder about the little boy. She helps me to a low couch and I lean back, close my eyes and start to track all the throbs and pains and notice I'm still feeling sick.

She doesn't ask me what happened, hardly speaks, except to say I mustn't sleep.

'I need to.'

'You might have a concussion.' She kneels in front of me and looks into my eyes, serious faced, searching. It's such a strange kind of looking; not at *me* but at my eyes just themselves and even in my pain I want her to see me. 'You can't sleep just yet.'

How does she know this? I wonder. But I keep quiet; words are hard to form, though the thoughts are there. She goes carefully about, soft footed, so unlike the hard-paced go she does at work. She sets a pan of water to boil on the stovetop, disappears and comes back with towels and cotton balls, something in a glass bottle.

'Reba…'

'Shh…' she says without looking at me, but she's soft, soft.

She kneels in front of me again and begins to clean me up. The warmth and pain on being touched makes me wince. I suck in a breath. Light-headed. Close my eyes.

'Shh…' she says again. I think her hand cradles my cheek, feather light holding me steady. The other holds a damp cotton ball, moves slow, slow, touching, pressing lifting away, returns again and I hear her breath catch as I wince again.

''S okay,' I mutter and feel blindly in the air wanting to make contact with her. My hand drops into my lap. I'm so tired. I hope she mistakes my stupid tears for the water she's washing me clean with.

'I'm so sorry,' she says, her voice so low I almost don't hear what she says. I don't understand but I try shaking my head. 'Cassidy? I'm going to have to take a look at you.' My head contracts with I don't understand; she's already doing that. 'I need to unbutton your shirt.'

Something tightens in me and she says, 'I know, I'm sorry, but I need to make sure you don't have any... maybe you don't understand how beat up you are?'

I try to laugh, but just air snorts through my nose. It ain't funny anyhow.

'Mama?' A croaky voice comes from the other side of the room and I feel her pull away fast and she stands. 'What are you doing?'

'It's okay, baby,' she says in a quiet voice and pads over to where her little boy stands in his PJ's, rumpled, blinking. He raises a hand to rub his belly and meets my look and stares.

'I'm helping my friend.' She crouches and strokes his hair. 'You remember Cassidy? He helped us after school, remember?' She lifts him up and holding him close says something about an accident.

'What kind of a accident?' He's craning his neck around his mama's shoulder to keep his eyes on me and I wonder if I should say a word, or raise a hand or do some such other, but I got nothing left in me and can feel myself on the edge. 'Does he need a am-blunce?'

'No, baby, I think I can take care of it.'

'You can take of care of everybody huh, Mama?'

They're through into the other room now and I can't hear her answer but I catch a low chuckle, their voices murmuring until she begins humming something low and familiar. I lay my head against the back of the couch and feel myself unravel and come apart.

The touch of her hand on my face brings me back with a jerk. I try to gather myself a little, wondering if she'll see how messed up I am, hoping she don't.

She leans down and asks me to open my eyes. 'Can you do that for me?' she says and something in the way she asks it for herself touches me. Everything's so raw. Must be the beating I took.

She looks into my eyes, so serious and unsmiling, looking for something she maybe don't want to see.

'Find what you're hunting for?' I ask her, trying again for light.

'Yes. No. I can't tell,' she says. 'I'm trying to see if your pupils are the same size. If you have a concussion. But your eyes are so swelled I can't tell.' She smiles a little. 'I still need to take a look at you. Did he have a weapon do you know?'

'Aside from them rings on his fingers?' I ask. 'Seemed like he had something on every damn one. Maybe could have held my own...' The shame at being whupped is rising inside me, or maybe it's that she's unbuttoning my shirt. Whatever it is it's got me running away at the mouth. 'If he hadn't of had a piece a metal on each finger, yeah, I'd maybe of come off a little better. You ever been beat up by a bunch a rings? Can't say I recommend it.'

She sucks in a breath like I myself just hurt her. 'What?' She's frozen still. Then she seems to shake herself alive again and says, 'Are you sure?' before answering for me. 'You're having the shit kicked out of you and you're counting rings? Give me a break.'

She starts working on me again and it takes me a minute while she's peeling back my open shirt, to realise she ain't just angry, she's scared. I'm uneasy by how slow on the uptake I feel myself to be.

'I'm sorry,' I tell her, not sure what I'm apologising for, but feeling the need and I lay back feeling spent.

'It's okay,' she murmurs, and her fingers, gentle, thorough, pass over my skin. I'm thankful for her care, but even so I'm chewing down pain with just about every testing pressure she makes, and I can tell that something's changed to make her scared but I don't know what. My brain's so slow, I can't finish a thought to its end. I start one up, then can't seem to hold to where it's headed.

She leaves me be and straightens up the room that don't need it except for my jacket thrown on the floor. She grabs it up.

'*Don't touch that!*' I tell her, so sharp that she curses and drops it. A bunch of stuff falls out of the pockets and I close my eyes all out of gas after that one holler.

Her voice comes, dry and a little mocking. 'Is it okay if I pick up your wallet and keys?'

'Of course,' I say, relieved that's all that fell out, hating my ungraciousness in the face of her kindness. She leaves everything where it's fallen and comes over, hands on her hips.

'Look here, Cassidy,' she says. 'It's nothing to me how you go about your business, okay? I don't give a damn. But you better tell me right now if I've brought anything into this house I shouldn't have, you got me? I have enough going on in my life without—I have a little boy to consider.'

I'm slow, but I think I understand her meaning. 'It's nothing like that,' I tell her. 'Do I look to you like I'm dealing, Reba?'

'People hardly ever look like what they are,' she says, voice hard.

Well amen to that. There's a long moment while she stands there, looking at me, eyes a little narrowed like she's making a calculation. At last she turns away and sets herself down in a chair by the window, looking out. She's tense and wired up.

Eyes closed, a question comes to me without my knowing it. 'You know who that was out there, don't you?' She says nothing and my head hurts so bad I can't be sure if the words came out or not. Maybe they're just swimming round my head along with the other stuff that's hot-footing it about in there, not making any sense.

'You have some serious bruising,' she says, from over by the two-seater dining table. 'It's deep I think. Maybe even some cracked ribs. You should probably have it checked out; I'd hate if I missed something.'

'Wouldn't be the first time,' I say, not wanting to go into the ER or anywhere else for that matter, but she don't respond and I try and open an eye to see what she's doing. Out the corner of that stupid swelled up eye, I see her stooped, picking up the last of my stuff that's fell out; my wallet and a bunch a loose change. She stands up and hangs my jacket on the back of a chair, but she ain't looking at that. She's holding my wallet how it's fell open and looking at the inside. I close my eyes and sink into myself, waiting for her question, but it don't come.

She's moving quietly about the place and I can hear the sounds of dishes being washed, fridge door opening and closing, the rustle of paper and I think, she's making that little boy a lunch box maybe and I remember doing the same for Petey sometimes. I feel my throat tighten so it hurts; I'm glad of the low light.

I drift... Reba's talking. On the phone. Her voice is whispered, angry, frightened. *'You promised... this again... last time...'* I want to understand what she's saying... can't hear when I'm floating... falling

How much time's passed I do not know. 'You should sleep,' I say, words thick in my mouth.

'I'm just going to watch you for a little while longer, make sure you're okay.' She's sitting in a chair by the window. If she's watching me, she's watching out the window too. She's so different to how I mostly see her, always on the move, hummingbird. Now, she's alert to everything, but still as a mountain lynx, waiting. I'm glad my eyes are swelled so I can watch her without she's thinking me strange. After a time, she turns the lamp out, whispers goodnight.

As I drift again, I realise I ain't thanked her and I mean to do it, but my words fall asleep on my tongue.

I wake in a wash of cold sweat, throat, mouth, stuffed full of fear and heartbeat. I try to sit and flip the light on to prove to myself I'm not standing outside the Walmart with a gun pressed into my neck; that in fact I'm in my van, in the barn in Beau's field by the creek, 186 miles from Mason County, but a wicked-sharp pain tears through me, and I realise that things ain't what they ought to be. I start to feel a rising panic, I can't figure out where in hell I am and ain't nowhere on my body that's not shouting at me.

I make myself breathe and slowly it comes to me, that I'm inside Reba's place, laying on a couch way too short in length for me. I try to get myself a little more comfortable and a sound comes from me like the pain I'm feeling. Long time since I woke so fearful. What was it? Flashback? Dream. Hard to say. Don't matter either, I guess. It is what it is.

They say that flashbacks and nightmares is what you get when you don't face a thing. Mama once told me Lucille's only brother was in the first Iraq war and came back so broken from what he seen or maybe done, she said, he ended up shooting himself in the head with his uncle's gun. She said he tried to pretend it hadn't happened and that's what done for him. 'You got to face things, sweetheart,' she'd tell me. 'First rule of life.' Well, that weren't the only advice I ended up ignoring.

'Cassidy?' Okay, so I am with Reba. That was definitely her voice from somewhere other side of the room. 'Can I get you something? Does it hurt?'

'Ain't you been to bed yet?'

'I am in bed,' she says, voice low. I hear the rustle of bed sheets and the little boy whimpers. 'It's okay, baby, shhh...' I hear the bed springs as she rustles again.

I picture her a few feet away, curled around her little boy while he sleeps and in the deep quiet of this strange night, I hear him breathing. It has a little whistle to it at the tail end of his out breath and just hearing it twists me up and wrenches me tight.

'How old is he? Your little boy?' It tumbles out of me.

'He's six years old.' There's something real sweet about the way she says it; like he's done something she can be proud of.

'My little... Petey, his name was. He was some younger. Still in preschool.'

Reba's sigh comes to me through the dark like it's a wind shifting through a bed of reeds. 'What happened to him?' she asks, so gentle I almost can't stand it. It takes me a while to answer and when I do, I know I sound cold.

'He died,' I tell her and her next sigh gets caught halfway.

'I knew there was something,' she says and I almost laugh at the smallness of that last word, the lone nature of it.

It's so dark it takes me by surprise when she sits down on the floor beside me. She's got a rug wrapped around her and she sits with her back against the couch, close to my shoulder. I can't tell if her eyes are open or closed, but I can smell her warmth and her hair loosed from them tight braids, is springing from her head and has fallen a little over where my hands lie clasped on my chest. In... out... breathe.

'I'm so sorry,' she says.

'It was my fault.' I don't know why I want her to know this, but I can't help myself.

Reba is very still, her breathing stays even. 'Somebody tell you that, or you know it to be true?'

'Both.'

The day I killed my little brother, was the day after Harper's twenty third birthday. I remember waking up late in the afternoon. It weren't really waking; it was more akin to coming round, coming to, which to be fair is most probably exactly what I was doing. The inside of my head felt bigger'n the skull that contained it and was pulsing and pushing to get out. My mouth was so dry, tongue so swelled it was fused shut.

No doubt, there would have been the short but blessed relief of not knowing where I was, nor who I was and in truth achieving that state had for weeks been my only focus. You could say that at that time, it was my full-time occupation, my life's work; doing whatever it took to smother every spark and flame of memory or feeling.

But as always, even in that suspended moment of nothing, I knew with sick certainty I'd remember, and I felt a terror rising in my craw that wouldn't be quelled. I threw it up over the side of my bed, bitter and stringy, but felt no better. Just empty. Empty. And I prayed for empty to stay.

Petey dying, was the last of everything that happened back home in Mason, before I finally realised that unless I got the hell out of there, and fast, more shit was going to happen, more hearts would get broke and I'd end up dead myself. Truth be told I had got to where I was ready to accept that as my rightful fate—hell, that's a straight up lie, it wasn't accepting, it was an out an out active wanting it to happen and doing as much as I could to help it along. Lord forgive me, but that's the truth.

'Reba,' I say her name and she turns her face towards mine. She looks puzzled.

'Do you see me?' She's so close; I can feel her breath warm against my face. 'Don't you know me?' I peer in her eyes remembering the way she looked into mine and saw what was in my soul all that time ago. 'I was on the way to his funeral. You... I... it was me you helped, at the memorial service.'

At first, I can see she don't know what I'm talking about, but then a dawning recognition rises in her face,

120

then pain, swallowed down—fear? I can't tell, and I'm frightened of what I might have done in telling her.

I see then that she did not know me, did not connect that raw mess of pain and fear and self-hating grief she held in her arms in the waffle house in Lexington, with me, Cassidy-behind-the-bar. It was only I who had remembered, who had recognised anybody. All these weeks I been thinking she was in it with me, sharing a secret. I liked to think she was doing it out of respect for me and I feel foolish. She just didn't remember. It almost hurts to think I made more of it than she and I feel alone, adrift again. Then I wonder, maybe I am more changed than I know. I ain't felt it, but then change can come slow, only those ain't been around you truly see it.

'You? But...' she reaches out then and the touch of her fingertips on my unshaved face make me flinch; it feels like she's touching *me* and it's too much. Strange, when she been with them same hands tending to me all over, not two hours before. She touches my hair and I take a hold of her hand to stop her, but end up holding onto it tight, like she's gon keep me anchored, cause I'm flying on my grief is what I'm doing and I'm afraid.

'You have no idea,' she says and she's shaking her head like she can't understand what she's seeing with her own eyes. 'You've been a ghost haunting me.' I don't hear the sense of her words, just feel her arms about my head, holding me to her like she done once before, only this time she's crying. She is. Reba.

I never made it to my little brother's funeral. Newspaper, local TV, and town folks were everywhere I went, muttering, shouting, turning their backs. I never knew till then what shunning meant, nor how it felt, but them as used to be friends, them as was neighbours turned their backs and fell silent as I approached. Bricks come through our windows and one morning, couple weeks after they winched the truck up from the gorge, somebody set light to our porch. I never could understand how Mama was being punished for something I done and I told her it'd be easier if I just didn't go to the funeral, at least that way she could mourn without folks looking at me. But she didn't understand.

'I'm *done* with how hard it is for you! I don't care anymore! I lost my baby! Because of you, I lost my child! You need to be there. You *face* it. If you'd faced up to what happened to Harper instead of hiding in the bottom of a bottle like that no-good father of yours, none of this would have happened!' Mama's voice, tearing into me. 'He was your brother; show some respect! He loved you.'

And I loved him. He was bright light and sunshine; yellow haired, a puzzled puppy dog of a face, always on the move. The only one who called me, '*John-John!*' Piped high through the yard whenever he was hunting me out for a romp, or a sandwich or a ride to the store for an ice cream.

He and his two little buddies liked to play in the truck. Firefighters. I knew that. Everybody knew it. It was their favourite game and Petey, he was set on joining the fire department when he was grown. Five years old and he knew what he wanted to do.

It was Lucille herself told me Mama'd be better off without me and I ain't dumb, I'd worked that out for myself some time before.

'Folks can't look at her without seeing you. You're bad blood, John C, you don't belong here anymore. Let your mama find some peace. She's loved here, but not so long as she harbours you.'

Ain't that a strange way to put it? Harbour. When it was my home is all, same as it ever had been.

'What's that?' Reba's voice cuts into my thoughts.

'Hmm?'

'You just said something about a harbour, your home.'

I didn't know that my words had came out. I wonder if the kicking's done worse to me than I know. 'I'm thinkin' about them days before you sheltered me. I guess it's messin' with my head a little.'

'Understandable,' she says. 'Loss like that, it can make you crazy.'

The way she says it, like she ain't meaning me, it reminds me of what we were both doing in the same place. It's dark and she's so close by. I have to say it.

'I seen you there, Reba, before you helped me. Outside the statehouse at the victims' memorial. You weren't no passer-by. You were there, holding a cut out. You were remembering someone.'

She moves back and the closeness I been feeling pulls away and hangs unsettled between us. I can almost hear the calculations whirring inside of her and I want to tell her she can trust me; I would if I thought it'd make a difference. 'Who were you honouring?'

She don't say anything for a long, slow breath. Then real abrupt, like she's jumping in before she can change her mind, she says, 'My sister.'

It hurts to hear, but there's something else too, a glad feeling of knowing her better, or more or something, which right away makes me real uncomfortable. I don't understand; I wouldn't wish that on anybody. I don't know what to say. Nothing anybody ever said to me ever made the blindest bit of difference, but even so all the same kind of things jump to my lips.

'I'm sorry,' I say, useless. Once more I am grateful for the darkness.

'And now,' she says as though I ain't said nothing at all. 'It's starting up all over again. I thought me and Sailor were safe, I'm supposed to be under witness protection but no one's really going to protect us but me.'

I get a sharp snag of apprehension and look to see what she means. Is she asking me something? But she ain't looking at me. She's got her knees pulled up under her chin, her arms wrapped tight around them, staring out into the darkness. I wish I had words of comfort, something to say that could make her feel safe, just for a moment, but I am the last person on earth to do that.

'I want to tell you something.' Reba's voice ain't as steady as I am accustomed to. 'Five years ago, Sailor's dad beat his mother so bad she died of it.'

I want her to stop talking for a minute; she ain't making sense. My head's hurting. 'He was released from jail on license a couple of weeks ago, but it seems he's cut off his tag.'

'That was the guy that jumped me?' It sounds like a question, but it ain't one. I know that's exactly what she thinks, but I'm still swirling around with Sailor's mother being so beat up she's dead. I know I'm being slow, but I can't match things up.

'I can't be certain, but it makes sense. I talked to the Lexington police tonight and they told me the last sighting they had, he was heading this way.' She's moved even further from me and I try and sit up better, but pain flies through me and I have to stop.

'Sailor... he's not—he's not your son?'

She shakes her head. 'No, but he's mine.' The way she says it is fierce, the Reba I know from work challenging me to say it ain't so. 'My sister,' she sounds softer now. 'She was going to lose him so I stepped in. It's all in law,' she says. 'Only, he—Sailor's father—he won't accept it. He can't stand that he doesn't have control and he has some kind of psychiatric report claiming that he isn't a danger to anyone else, the circumstances between him and my sister were unique and are unlikely to happen again.'

I am reminded of them that said the same about Grady. That Harper provoked him. That he was a nice guy. That any red-blooded male faced with what he was, might have done the same. I close my eyes. I think about how she and

124

Sailor was okay until Brooke arrived and for the first time I wonder who tipped her off. Who told Brooke that the two people in the Waffle House Waitress in *Random Act of Kindness* video was us? Who told her where to find us?

'Reba,' I say again. 'I don't know what all's got stirred up, but I am sorry for my part in it.' And I'm thinking, if I just give Brooke Adler her story, maybe that'll be enough for her to lay off of Reba.

'Look,' I say, hoping it comes out right. 'If you ever need a place...' I hate to say hide. Why should she have to hide? 'A place to stay, somewhere out of the way, there's always my van.'

'I wouldn't know where to find it,' she says, almost as if she wouldn't care to. But I sketch her a little map and watch as she tucks the folded paper in the edge of a mirror by the front door. Somehow this makes me a little easier.

Some days have spent themselves without I really noticed them, aside from Beau appearing out of nowhere to take me to his place. I guessed Reba to have called him, but I didn't have the energy to ask.

'You think nobody's going to notice if you don't show your face?' he says when he arrives and helps me out of the apartment.

The strangeness of leaning on an old man causes me to hold back, but his wiry arm feels good and strong and he locks it about me; I take his help.

'Lark was about to lose her mind with worry.' Belle's come with him and she just give me a look like it were my life's mission to upset everybody.

Lark. I hadn't thought of her in all the time I was at Reba's and it shames me. She's a good girl; a good friend to me. Of course she would've noticed and it was she who thought of calling Reba when I didn't appear at work.

'But I don't think she was expecting you to *be* there,' Belle says, a little brine in her voice. 'Oh that poor girl, I don't know.'

A shot of anger launches itself through me at Lark. Why at her, I can't say, but I do not want to have to think about her worrying about me and how I am the cause of it. I don't want it. Like a kid, all I want to do is kick out something stupid like, she don't own me or some other dumb-ass thing like that, but I bite it. I look back at the door, in part to see if Reba picks up on this, but she's already inside and closed the door.

'Come on now, sugar,' Beau's coaxing Belle. 'Looks to me like he's been kicked enough for now. You can carry on all you like later.' He gets a laugh out of her anyhow and she tells me she's sorry.

'I didn't mean to get ugly,' she says, 'but Beau will tell you I'm one of those who scratches when the danger's over. Glad you're safe, hon.'

I told you she was a sweetheart.

Beau, he chuckles, deep and dark and pulls his truck out onto the road. Belle's sitting between us and her thick perfume and the glare of the sun angling off of the snow is making my head ache worse. Every bump and hitch sends aftershocks through my frame and I wonder, maybe I ain't going to make this journey without we'll have to pull over. Wish I was walking.

'So, did you decide about Thursday?'

I take it that Beau's talking to Belle and she answers right away, but turns to me. 'What do you think, hon?' she pats my hand and I flinch. She and I both notice and I try and smile, it's okay. 'I keep wanting to put off this month's Porch Lies...'

'Why would you do that, Belle? Folks look forward to it,' I say.

'Your mama ever tell you not to interrupt? I was getting to that.'

I smile and stare back out the window. 'Don't blame my mama if I turned out bad,' I say and they laugh.

'I don't trust that woman from KYTV.' Belle says and I'm surprised; she's sure changed her tune since I last saw her giving Brooke Adler the inside story. 'She's recording and filming every time you turn around. That damn microphone in somebody's face noon and night.' Belle's picking up speed and sounds real out of joint. 'Getting a feel for the community, she says, building trust, she says. Foot.' That makes me smile. You know Belle's fit to bust when she hauls out the old timey cuss words.

'How do you know she don't mean it?' I ask her, devil in me playing up.

'*Cassidy*!' she just about hollers and Beau makes a wincing, hissing through his teeth. 'You of all people saw through her the moment she arrived, so don't start.'

Is that what Belle thinks? That I saw through Brooke? I'd like to think so, but truth be told, she just put the wind up me big time.

Belle goes on, worrying that folks will feel hog-tied by Brooke being there, worrying she'll somehow spoil the intimacy and community trust she, Belle, has built up over time. Like I said, folks enjoy Porch Lies, but they use it as a confessional too, purge their pain, share their joys and foolishness's, their hopes and dreams and they know, or at least hope, ain't nobody going to hold it against em. That's right, they save that for the TV shows, play judge and jury both, loud as they can, thinking nobody gets hurt.

I lean back and close my eyes and think about Reba. I think about her hair, colour of beech and maple leaves in the fall, them troubled grey eyes that soften when she hears Sailor call. And I think about how her questions had me slipping back in my mind to the mountains of my home and everything that gets in the way of remembering it to be anything other than a dark and hopeless place.

What happened? I didn't know how to answer her. I don't know now. To tell the story would be less than what happened. I want to tell it so it's understood, so I understand. Maybe Belle was right when she said I should tell my story. It's how we make sense of things, Cassidy, she always tells me. But maybe some things don't never make sense.

Reba's manner changed when Beau arrived to take me home. No, not so. It was when he called to say he was on his way and the tender feeling in the space between us disappeared until all there was, was the space. It felt to me as though what we'd shared was just in my imaginings.

And all at once I'm minded of Harper long ago, shrugging herself out of my arms, still damp and slick with sweat, eyes refusing to meet mine and how in that moment, all the heat and hope and feeling of homecoming I'd felt, had turned chill.

'John? This doesn't change anything, okay? I'm still with Grady.' She let herself look at me then and I could see right away that she wished she hadn't. I don't want this to be what I remember of her, but it's running on a loop I can't stop. 'It's just sex, is all, it doesn't mean anything.'

'I know,' I said, not knowing any such thing.

Someone's banging hard on the barn door. How long they been at it, I can't tell; I feel like I'm being jerked by the collar rough and hard out of a black sleep. I need to get up and answer it but somehow, I'm minded not to. I don't know why.

The banging comes again, rattling the hinges and chain and is accompanied now by hollers telling me it's the cops. I holler back that I'm on my way, but I doubt that they can hear me through the muffle of the hay bales and my van.

I wonder at their patience while I'm fumbling with the chain and when I finally get it unlocked and swing open the barn door, squint and wince back from the sudden glare of the brightest of winter days, I wonder at them still being there.

The thing about cops is, I never can seem to trust a smiling one. Always feels like they're messing with you; waiting on you to mess up, let your guard down, then bam they have you.

There's two of them. A sober-faced woman, small and padded out in her bulletproof vest, and, standing a little behind, a big guy I seen around Levi's from time to time. He nods a recognition and says, 'Good morning sir. You are Cassidy McArthur?'

I nod and hang hard in the doorway, not moving either way. He peers around me into the dark barn behind.

'Got yourself quite the hideaway, haven't you, sir? We weren't sure this was the right place, were we?' He turns to his buddy and she shakes her head.

'Sir,' she says. 'Do you keep that chained up like that at night behind you?'

'I do ever since I had prowlers,' I tell her.

'Where's your fire escape, sir?'

I know I'm looking at her blank, like a fool; I'm surprised this is it what they come out here for.

But then she changes tack and says, 'Mr McArthur sir, we've had a report that you were the victim of an assault two weeks ago, correct?'

I nod and feel uneasy; on the back foot. Does Reba know they're here? Is it safe to talk?

'Can I ask why you didn't report it yourself, sir?'

'There weren't no point. I didn't see the guy and I guess I ended up okay.'

They exchange a look and my unease ratchets up. My mouth feels dry.

'You didn't see him? Are you sure?' I shake my head. 'But you're certain it was a male?'

I laugh at that. Perhaps out of place, but it just comes like a shot, short and hard.

'Yeah… no doubt about that.'

'Sir, would you mind coming down to the station and giving us a statement? And while you're there, if you could just take a look at the line up and see if you can ID him? We've picked up a suspect.'

I'm shaking my head now. 'I already said. I didn't see him, what good would it…'

In my head I'm backing away and thinking it ain't my business. I want nothing to do with them or him or ID parades. And then the woman police officer, she says something that changes my mind.

'It sure would help us if you could just try. Otherwise this fella's just going out there and beat up somebody else and next time they might not be as lucky as you were. We've already got one positive ID.'

I'm about to say no one else was there, how could they have, but I shut my mouth and wonder about Reba that night. What did she see or hear? She could have seen the whole damn thing. Noise could easily have woke her, not that it matters, she couldn't have done nothing anyhow without putting herself and the boy in danger.

I'm about to tell her again I saw nothing, but bits start coming to me; the smell of him, the leather and rings all over his hands, so I tell her I'll give it a go. Statement at least.

I ask them to give me a moment and duck into my van to throw on the rest of my clothes. I pull on my jacket and just as I slip my hand inside my pocket and feel for my box I think, I cannot take this into a police station. I don't want the smallest chance of anybody's hands being on this but mine. I close my fingers around the fine-grained wood, rubbing my thumb back and forth along the edge of the tiny trap door. I can feel the sticky curl of duct tape where the seal had started to come loose on account of my constant worrying at it, day after day as the miles stretched and the road took me far from home.

It's stayed taped up like that for too long, even though I always meant to get it fixed right one day. It fills me with shame and makes me sadder than ever; if I'd never took it, it would still be up on that mantle, no scratches, no bumps, and it sure as hell wouldn't be held together with a dirty little piece of Alabama chrome.

All the way to the station, riding in back of the cop car, all I can think of is that little wooden box, tucked under the bench in my van, behind my shoebox. Without it in my pocket, I find my thumb is rubbing across the pads of my fingers, over and over, until the woman officer looks in the rearview mirror at me and says, no need to be nervous, sir, this is just routine. Whatever. Her words do nothing to stop my throat from trembling like the leaves of a cottonwood.

Down at the station, they give me a cup of coffee and a book of mug shots to look at. And what a scene that is; desperate and dog tired most of em look.

Police officer starts to take my statement and I'm curious how she goes about it; questions that prompt my memory, but don't seem to have an agenda. She's good. I start to remember things I didn't know I'd noticed. It all happened so fast and he came at me from behind, but strange to say I know he was tall and big and I remember the rings. I still got the marks on me.

'So, you finished work at…' I try and recollect the time and tell her it varies night to night, depending. I try hard to pin a time, but somehow just can't seem to do it.

'Try and be as specific as you can, sir. Alibis, you know?'

I wish I'd asked Reba, talked it over with her a little more. I'd hate to contradict her and get in the way of keeping her and Sailor safe. I think about what usually happens, how oftentimes it's after one in the morning before I'm headed home and I'm about to settle on sometime between one and two a.m. when I remember, that was the night Brooke told Lark about what I done.

'I left early that night,' I say. 'So, I reckon it was somewhere in the region of eleven thirty, maybe midnight.'

I recount how I found myself outside Reba's house and feel myself colouring and heating up, real uncomfortable. I shrug off my jacket and the police officer, she looks at me close, searching my face, giving nothing away.

'It's okay, sir, we just need to know about the assault.'

I tell her how it came out of nowhere and like I said, her questions are clever and she gets me thinking about how his voice sounded, what he'd said and if I remembered anything he was wearing. So I tell her about the rings and his leather jacket; that I'm certain it was black and well worn. Other details come to me. I could tell from the feel of his face against the side of my head when he first grabbed me from behind that he was clean shaven. His voice... I close my eyes and think, now where've I heard that voice before? Because as sure as anything, I know that I have and it weren't all that long ago.

'He was tall. Taller'n me,' I say. 'Bigger too. Big fella for sure.'

She raises her eyebrows. 'Do you know your height?'

'Six feet, thereabouts,' I say.

'And you say he was taller than you? What makes you say that?'

I explain how he came around me from behind, how he used his head to push mine sideways while he held me in an arm lock. She waits for a minute then says, 'And then he left you for dead?'

'Oh, I don't know about that,' I say, trying to lighten things up. 'I think he was warning me more'n trying to kill me. Or...' I stop and she nods for me to go on. 'Warning Reba, I think. Frightening her. Deliberate.'

She nods again then tells me we're done and if I'd just read through the statement and sign it, I can come and take a look at the line-up. She says it like it's a reward. I start to protest and she says it won't take long, then I'll be free to go.

I spot him right away and that surprises the fuck out of me. How can I identify someone I swear I didn't see? And is it right to ID someone because you suddenly remember the sound of a voice? But there he is, tall, broad, sure of himself, hands full of rings. Same guy that come in the bar asking me to settle an argument for him and his buddies.

When I get back, first thing I do is find my box. Just the feel of it calms me. I hold it in my palm, smooth at it with my thumb, but I am struck by indecision. What should I do? I wonder, like I done a hundred times before, if maybe it ain't right to carry it around with me all the time. After a while, I put it back in the shoebox with the news clippings and try to sleep.

Back at work, as the pain dulls and the bruising turns colour, an almost constant jarring and flipping inside of me takes over. Shadows bother me, sudden movements raise my pulse in an instant and take long, long moments to slow downward and sink back to normal. I can't settle, can't sit quiet and nothing but walking out in the woods can still my agitation for more'n a short time. I spend time in my head persuading myself that a drink is not the answer, but I'm real scared that I think it is. And worse even than that, I feel so full of held-tight rage, I'm afraid of myself.

I'm pulling a local brew for Freak, while Belle sets up against the far wall for this month's Porch Lies. Most often I look forward to it, even if Belle does make it her business to keep on at me about telling a story. But tonight, I'm full of jitters and have a heavy sense of something bad about to happen, but I can't tell what. It's November and Thanksgiving's coming up. Belle has the porch rocker set facing out into the bar, rigged out in pumpkins and candlelight and the theme she's chosen is Home. More people, she tells us, travel home for Thanksgiving than at any other time of year. But what of all them that have no place to travel to? I ask her.

'We'll see,' she says. 'Won't we?'

As is always, we don't know who's gearing up to tell a tale, or spin yarn; the idea is, the spirit moves you. For the first time since I took this job and decided to wait on fixing my van, I don't want to be around for it, but I don't know why.

I catch Freak's eye and right away regret it; in the secretive lighting of a beer joint like this, most folks have, so far, been missing my swelled face and residue of a black eye. They're squinting at me, some a them, thinking they've seen something, but I'm turned away before they can check.

'Jeez, man, you do not look good!'

I keep my eyes on the foaming head rising to the top of the glass and bite down hard for a minute before I open my mouth to answer. 'Thanks, buddy.'

He laughs. 'What happened to you?' While I make change, I tell him, without detail. 'Goes to show, goes to show...' he says. 'I never took you for the fighting type.'

'Freak,' I say, painstaking in my tone. 'I ain't. I told you, some asshole jumped me.'

'Well what for?' he asks. 'It definitely wasn't for your money!' He laughs like he's made an award-winning joke. 'Everybody about here knows you got nothing.'

'Well thank you for that, Freak,' I say. 'But in consideration of the fact that we are a recognised and registered distressed county, you could say that of just about anybody, so my guess is he's just an asshole.' I hope he drops it. He doesn't.

He puts his head on one side and says a little louder, 'Place your bets, people!' He bangs his hand on the bar and calls out, 'Who's been picking fights with our esteemed barkeep, and why?'

My insides curl, but I flash a smile at him, keep him sweet. 'Give it up, Freak,' I tell him and I try to keep my voice light, make like I don't care that he's ragging on me, but it's getting harder by the day to keep everything I'm feeling out of my voice. All at once I have an idea that I realise has been swimming about waiting for the right moment.

'Freak?' I rinse out a number of glasses and rack them in the washer. 'You still interested in that vinyl collection a mine?'

He give me look as though he's waiting on a mean ol' punch line at his expense. 'In what sense?' he asks, wary but interested.

'You still want to take a look? See if it's of any interest to you or any a them collectors you run into?'

Freak, he don't answer right away. In fact when he does speak, it makes me think he's smarter than he lets on.

'What's changed?'

I smile. 'Nothing. That's the problem. I don't seem to make enough here to fix my van and I'm getting about ready to move on.'

'Well, I can't make any promises. Mostly these things are worthless, but once in a while... that's part of the fun.' He give me a long look. 'Did I hear that there's some old blues records in there?'

'I don't know,' I keep it vague. 'Take a look, you're the expert.'

He says he'll swing by sometime in the week and as I turn to close the washer door and set it to run, I catch Beau's eye.

'You thought this through, Cassidy? Don't make any rash decisions just now. You've had more than a number of

135

hits in the last couple weeks.' I don't like the way he's looking at me like I'm a kid needs reigning in. I shrug. 'Sit on it for a while. A man should never let his only safety net go, unless it's the only thing left for him to do.'

I choose not to respond to Beau's unasked for advice and answer someone's holler from behind him, wondering what it takes to get a drink around here. Nothing new under the sun.

I'm working on autopilot, my mind chewing away about what to do, does any of it matter and why I ain't seen Reba. It's been some days since I was in her apartment and I can't lie, I'm non-stop thinking about her. Ever since she pulled a gun on me, thinking I was a prowler—and I guess I was from where she was standing—I been carrying an unshakeable fear that some terrible happening will come about on account of that gun and now that I know there's someone with hate in his heart watching her, it just about slays me every time I think about it. And that little boy in the house too.

Each time the door from the street opens, or I hear someone running up the back stairs from the kitchen, my belly gets to tightening and I keep thinking it could be Reba's coming in, but it never is and I start wondering what she's doing about money, about food. It jumps into my head then that maybe she just lit out and ain't in town no more, and man that is not a thought I like. I look about for Levi to ask him if she still works here, but I can't see him.

Walking home I tap my empty pocket and feel hollow and sad. Back at the van the lights are on. I don't even need to remind myself that I don't ever leave a light burning. I reach for a wooden pole and take a few steps in then stop. I am suddenly more tired than scared. My life. For a while there, I'd stopped watching my back every god damned minute of the day. Fuck it.

'*Who's in there?*'

There's a jump and a crash and a child's voice cries out and is shushed and my body from the inside out hisses, deflates and rests a little.

The door cracks and in the light coming from inside, Reba's curls glow about her head. I can't see her face.

'Cassidy, it's me. I'm sorry. I didn't know where else to go.'

I'm in front of her without even knowing how I cross the barn floor and almost reach to take her in my arms but stop myself just in time. I throw the pole aside and touch her light on the arm.

'What's going on?' I ask and I feel warm that she thought of me, that I might seem like a safe person to her.

She steps aside and I see she's made up the bed and Sailor is scrubby eyed and looking out from under the blanket like a frightened critter.

'Hey,' I say, trying to sound like this happens every day. 'How're you doin, Sailor?' he gives me a tiny nod and I wonder what Reba's doing dragging him all over. Then I feel like a heel for judging her.

'What's going on?' I ask her again.

'I can't stay in my house.' She glances at Sailor before going on in a lower voice. 'He's there, I know, watching me.'

'Did you call the cops? They're surely looking for him. They came and talked to me while I was at Beau's.'

'They haven't helped much so far. They just tell me to renew the protection order...' She breaks off. 'Do you have any idea how many times I've renewed it? It doesn't make a bit of difference, he keeps phoning and threatening and posting horrible things on Facebook. It's terrifying.' Her voice cracks and I reach out to her, hold her hand. It's limp in mine and after a moment I let it go.

'I didn't know they'd spoken to you.'

I nod. 'Yeah, they come down and took my statement. What'd they say?'

137

'I told them I'm too scared to stay there while they locate him and they gave me the name of a crisis centre, but it's miles away, and they don't have any space.' She gives me the fury look, like I might have made it so, and asks if I know three centres have been closed in the last year. 'They have twelve spaces serving four counties, it's crazy...'

In the quiet, I look around my van and wonder how it's going to work without sounding a loud 'listen-up' to everybody in town. I think of Lark and push it away fast; surely she'd understand.

'Cassidy, I'm sorry if this is difficult for you,' she starts to get up. 'I can go tomorrow, I just—I didn't think, I'm sorry. I... is there some... I've just thought, you might have a girlfriend. I hope I don't cause any trouble.' Her eyes cloud over and it's all I can do not to hold her, but I know she don't want that from me right now, maybe not ever.

'Tha's okay, Reba. You ain't no trouble to me.' I'm glad you thought of me, I think. 'I'll do what I can. You'll be safe enough here until we think of a plan.' But right away I wonder who in hell I think I am to say such a thing when I ain't never been able to keep that promise before.

If I had any brains, I'd be able to think of a real person who could truly help her, keep her and the youngin safe, instead of putting myself up as a one-man-lone-rider.

I lay awake on the pullout, alongside Reba and Sailor, but sleep don't come to me. All I can think of on a loop, is a hot summer night in a Walmart parking lot, loaded down with new-born disposable diapers and a flat-pack crib, a gun pressed into my throat and Grady Epp hollering to keep my eyes open or he'll shoot me there and then because I need to *watch* what happens to people who disrespect him.

It seemed to me at the time that Grady was more bent out of shape by what folks in the community thought of him losing Harper to another man, than he did about Harper leaving him. Especially when that other man was me.

'You're not man enough for her,' he used to say, way back when we was kids in high school and she had started running with him and his crowd.

He'd talk ugly about her and what all she let him do to her and how I weren't nothing but a fag who never would be good enough for her.

I never could find words to answer him and that'd make him laugh louder. 'Hit the nail right on the head there, didn't I? She laughs at you, John C., we all do. Think about that. She's laughing behind your back.'

What nobody understood was that I didn't give a hoot about that; Harper'd always been laughing at me, she laughed at everybody. It was her way. But what bothers folks for themselves they'll always put on somebody else. No imagination maybe. Anyhow, them as thought they knew it all but never once asked me about it, were certain in their minds that it must have been a contributing factor to what they all told was a show down between me and him.

In the end, I couldn't keep my eyes open and didn't care if he killed me then anyhow; as soon as he hit her, everything ended for me.

Reba reaches across the narrow space between us and holds my hand. 'Are you okay?'

'Sure,' I say. Then right away out comes the truth. 'No.' No, I am not okay. I am not. She knows not to ask anything more. She lifts my hand to her mouth and kisses it, and her lips feel dry and warm on my skin. She turns away then, so she's curled around Sailor, and tucks my hand under her chin. She falls into sleep almost at once and I am left with my memories, rising up and over and rushing on like spring melt into the creek below.

In the days that followed Harper's killing it was me too was dead. Six days after I'd squalled into the emergency room, running alongside her gurney, begging her to hold on, begging her, telling her over and over how sorry I was I didn't protect her, I walked, dead, out of the hospital.

I found I was home, Mama sitting on a kitchen chair in front of me asking what had happened. She'd sent Petey over to his little buddy's house for a few days so he didn't have to hear all about it, but it didn't matter; all I could say was that I couldn't remember. It weren't that, though. What she didn't understand was that I couldn't speak it; I could not bear witness to what I'd seen.

'How? *How* can you not remember?'

I can still see her face twisted with confusion and disbelief and it's only coming to me now that what she didn't understand, she couldn't believe.

'I remember coming out a the Walmart,' I told her and then stopped. It was as far as I could get and her face said to me, you're holding something back while out loud she said, 'Unless you tell me what happened, I can't help you.'

Those were familiar words; if ever I got into trouble at school, that's what she'd say and sure enough if ever I missed an important, shameful detail and she learned of it, I was on my own.

'I'm telling you,' I said, dry eyed, throat like husks. 'Like I told the police come to see us up at the hospital. I can't remember what... how... Grady was there and he had him a gun and there was a lot a shoutin' and hollerin' and...' but I couldn't go on and felt choked on what I couldn't say.

Then she asked me something the cops too had asked and in time Harper's own family, even her no-good-disappeared-mama who re-emerged looking for her place in the sun, when the local newspapers made something of it all, dolled up for the photos like she was auditioning for a part in a show.

'Why? How? I don't understand. You must have… *What did you do?* No one just pulls a gun out and shoots somebody for no reason.'

But here's the thing, sometimes they do. And tell me this, if there is a reason, does that make sense of it? What reason in all the world could there be that would give sense to a thing like that?

Looking at my mama then, I thought that if she didn't understand me nobody would. I never felt so lonely in all my life.

I can hear the soft, sleep sounds from Reba and her little boy and I'm more awake than I've ever been. Something that's been worrying and worrying at me like a dog with a bone takes on a shape I'm surprised I ain't thought of before. I been laying there thinking about the newspapers and the TV crews coming to tell just another story about a girl killed by her violent ex and all this time I been wondering why Brooke takes such an interest in this particular story when there's so many others. And I never even done the most basic thing; I never asked her why.

Lark always says people only ask the questions they're ready to hear the answers to. Now, I'm not sure I would agree with that on account of seeing so many folks get bent right out of joint when they get an answer, but anyhow I didn't ask Brooke. I just didn't.

In the ordinary way of things when I can't sleep, I get up and do something; draw, listen to something, maybe even read, but I don't want to wake Reba, nor Sailor, so I lay there, trying hard as I can not to think, not to remember, but that makes me think of Harper crying, 'I'm sick of people telling me not to think about it!' As if Grady's threats were just an ugly thought. 'And anyhow,' she'd say, 'everybody knows if someone tells you not to think of blue elephants, that's the only damn thing you're going to think about!'

Sometimes I'd think up more stupid or outlandish things not to think about and she'd stop crying and cussing and laugh, but it weren't no guarantee. Nothing was. And I miss you. I miss you. I miss you.

'Can't you sleep?' Reba's voice comes to me in a whisper.

I take in a breath, hard as I can, pull myself together and tell her I'm sorry. 'I ain't never been much of a sleeper,' I say. 'Well. Maybe years ago before...' I trail off and she tells me I got no business saying sorry.

'We've crashed your home, Cassidy. It's me who should be apologising.'

I shrug, try and make myself laugh; it come out like some kind of coughing. I shake myself out and stand.

In the van, filled as it is with Reba and the boy, I feel myself huge and clumsy and pointless. She come here for safety and I'm flailing about in the middle of the night and acting like a crazy.

'I sure am sorry I woke you.'

She sits up, delicate, and Sailor don't even stir.

'You want to tell me what's on your mind? I'm awake now too.' She says it with a bit of humour, for which I am grateful. I go to something else that's been on my mind; I can't talk about Harper now.

'Reba, do you think Belle's right? That stories need telling?'

Reba sits back against the pillows and I see how she strokes Sailor's hair, light and repetitive; I wonder if she even knows she's doing it.

She gives a tiny shrug. 'I don't know, why?'

'I think might be you do. The Silent Witness memorial every year? You're honouring your sister for sure, but everybody there is telling somebody else's story.'

She doesn't say anything, but looks at me, quiet and steady.

I crouch and sweep my hand under the bench, so it hits up against the edges of my old shoebox and I pull it out.

I put the box on my lap and tap the lid. 'I got some old news clippings from the time Petey was killed. I don't know why I keep them, but every time I turned around somebody was at me to tell them what happened, how it happened, and I couldn't say. I thought these might help.'

'Did they?'

I shrug. 'I couldn't read them for the longest time. Then all I could think was, it weren't you was there. You don't know how it was.'

Reba don't speak, but she's soothing to me; her listening ways; her quiet. She's different at work.

'Reba? You still working at the bar?'

She shakes her head. 'I can't. I'm scared Sailor's dad's going to come in there again.'

'You moving on?'

She nods.

'Where are you thinking of goin?' I don't ask her if she has any family, she told me her sister was killed and no doubt if she had any family to speak of she'd already have thought of that.

'In my dreams, Cassidy, or for real?' she asks and that makes me so sad to hear I don't say a word. She half laughs, a quiet snort and says, 'I've spent the last three years trying to keep Sailor and myself safe and... you can't rest. I'd like to get somewhere where I can take a rest from all this. That's all.'

I think of Harper and me living with the always hanging fear Grady was going to turn up. I think of how upside down the world is, where someone terrorising you gets to stay put while the terrorised is told to move on, get out, leave your home; shunned, by your own for what some other asshole is doing to you.

'Y'all are just asking for trouble staying around here,' Lucille was always happy to say. 'It's just like you want to rub Grady Epp's nose in it. That boy was always trouble. I never did understand why you went and got yourself mixed up with him in the first place. I told...'

'*Yeah, right!*' This line of talk always got to Harper and no wonder. 'If you hadn't have been wasted half the time, maybe you'd have noticed before it was too late.'

Then Lucille would raise her hand to whup her and Harper'd jump back always ready and laugh at her granmaw and always, Lucille, she'd somehow let it go.

'I'm too old for all this,' she'd say, though she weren't but a few years older'n my Mama. 'Don't say I didn't warn you.'

When Harper reported Grady to the police, they were sympathetic as could be, but advice was the same.

'Sweetheart,' the local police officer told her—same one as had hauled her ass in for running with Grady and his buddies, wild as she was, and given her a second chance. 'You be better off making a fresh start somewhere new.' He'd wished her well, told her the number to call—again— if Grady appeared on Mama's property and said he'd pay him a call.

'Between you and me,' he said to me, 'I'm not disputing that the guy is a douchebag,' and he laughed like we was old friends. 'But there's nothing I can do about a photo on Facebook. Anyhow, he's just out of joint because he lost his girl.' He winked at Harper. 'And who can blame the guy, right? You all go on home, try not to think about it and you call any time if you need us, okay? We'll be there.'

But anybody with an eye that's looking can see what Grady meant by uploading a picture of himself with his firearms titled 'when you least expect it.'

'Reba?'

'What is it, Cassidy?' She sounds tired.

'I want to help you. You and Sailor. I got me a little money put aside for fixing my van. I can take you two someplace.' I move a little closer to her.

She rustles about setting Sailor down alongside her where he's fallen asleep again and sits up higher. She has that fierce look, her eyes snapping. I can almost hear what's in her head so before it comes out I go on, 'I know you can take care of yourself, you been doin' it and you can keep on doin' it, I don't doubt you. But there ain't no shame in taking help from a friend, Reba.'

She starts to speak and looks even more fired up, 'Is that all you want? To help a *friend*?' The way she presses on that last word makes me twist inside with shame and confusion. Didn't she come here by herself looking for my help? How is this any different?

'I ain't asking for anything in return, Reba. Why would you think that?' I can't understand why I burn as I say it.

She looks as though I'm the town fool again. 'Why would I...' she breaks off and takes a breath. 'I'm sorry,' she says. 'That wasn't fair.' Her voice is flat. 'No doubt you meant it kindly...'

But the words have been said and I can't look at her. I get up and put on my outdoor things, trying to keep as quiet as I can on account of Sailor.

'What are you doing?'

'I can't sleep, Reba, all I'm doing is disturbing you and the youngin. I'm gon take a walk.'

She tries to make me change my mind, but I let her know I do this all the time; she's not to make anything out of it.

'Well that's ridiculous,' she says. 'I make insulting assumptions about your kind-hearted intentions and I shouldn't read anything into you hoofing it out into the dark?' Somehow, her tone, it makes me smile.

'Just quit, Reba, and get some sleep.' I smile at her to make her feel better and head out before she can say more.

145

It's a hard, cold, night, but ain't as bitter as it's been and I warm up pretty quick with the walking. There's a thin snow on the ground and the black earth is showing through in places; reminder that it's there.

I get to thinking about Harper and how she came to me and Mama, remembering how things had been when we was kids, and hoping we would take her in. A thought comes to me that I know I've fought off forever. If there'd been somewhere for Harper, like that shelter Brooke Adler talked about on her show, maybe she would never have come to me. It weren't me she was wanting or needing, but somewhere safe to rest a while.

The day she came it was a hot, spring morning. Petey and me, we'd filled a pan with water and I was sitting on the porch watching for the first hummingbirds. Mama'd put out sugar water coloured red in hanging tubes around the eaves and Petey swore he'd seen one that very morning. But he was always saying it, wanting it to be him that caught the first sighting.

He'd just pulled up a chair and hauled the Birds of America book out onto the porch, dragging it along beside him, scuffing the dustjacket in a way like to have made Mama crazy. We was looking through for Hummingbirds and the ones we were likely to see around these parts.

'Where do we have to be to see one a these, John-John?'

'Oh, way out West, Petey. You ain't gon set your eyes on Anna's Hummingbird unless you find yourself almost in California,' I told him.

'Can you take me there? Can we go there?'

'Sure we can, Petey. When d'you want a go? This afternoon? After you take your nap?'

Petey had a look he'd give me when he wasn't certain if I was messing with him or not; I can picture it to this day. He was doing that face when I heard the sound of wheels on the gravel road that sloped sharp up to our front yard.

At first, I couldn't make out who it was getting out of the truck. The sun was at an angle slanting through the trees along the ridge right into my eyes so it was impossible even to see the vehicle. Whoever was driving, seemed almost to toss the passenger out, along with a couple bags and turn right around, throwing up a cloud of dust while they done it.

I stood and shaded my eyes, just as Petey gave a little yelp and ran down the porch steps, calling out, '*Harper!*'

Even now I can recall the hot, raw feel in my chest when I realised it was her. I hadn't seen her to speak to since she'd told me what we done together was just sex, it meant nothing. Now here she was, and I couldn't think why. I had dreamed of her so often and so dirty I felt myself burning up as though she'd see it writ all over me and for a moment I just stayed where I was.

'John C? You just going to stand there like a goober?' she called out, which made me smile and I walked slowly over, trying to keep steady more'n anything else. She looked up at me from where she was bent giving Petey a hug and my head just about exploded.

'Jesus Christ, Harper...' I didn't need to ask her who done it. I felt sick to my stomach and all I could do was stand there while Petey babbled about Harper taking a fall.

'What kind of a fall done that to you?' I asked her and the look she gave me choked my words off. Her eyes filled with tears.

'I need a place to stay.' She reached out a hand. 'Just for a little while. Is Summer about?'

I took her hand, loving that she'd reached out to me like that, and helped her up. She kept hold of me.

'Mama's at work,' I said, trying to sound relaxed. 'But come on in. She won't mind putting you up for a while, you know that.'

'It won't be for long, John, just while I get things straightened out.'

'Sure.'

I didn't ask about Lucille; it'd been all over town that she'd washed her hands of Harper after she and Grady had snuck into her home when she was out of town and took a bunch of stuff Harper said her own mama'd meant for her, but I had no way of telling if that was for real.

There was so much I wanted to ask her, but it went out the window when she stood up straight. There weren't no mistaking the shape and swell of her belly and she caught my look right away.

'Yeah…' She laughed, but she was crying too. 'I'm pregnant.'

'Petey, go on inside and get Harper some iced tea, buddy.'

We sat on the porch steps together and I ain't never seen Harper like it. She just about fell apart and I held her together.

'I'm such a fuck up, John,' she said, crying hard and leaning into me. 'I don't even know whose baby it is. Could be you, could be him. What kind of a start is that? I guess everybody was right about me, I turned out just like they said.'

She told me she'd made a mess of everything, how scared she was; of Grady, of being a mama, of being alone, of having no home and I told her none of it mattered.

'It's okay, it'll be alright. I'll take care of you, Harper. You know that's all I ever wanted.'

She held onto me and I to her and I couldn't tell whose tears were whose.

Mama was sweet as can be to Harper's face, but after a few days she took me aside and gave me some tough talk.

'John, since when did you start believing in fairy stories?' I started to answer but she weren't interested in what I had to say. 'Lord knows I love that girl like she was my own, but if she thinks I'm going to stand by while she tries to pass that baby off as yours, she's crazier than I thought. Does she think folks don't know how babies are made?'

'There's a chance it *is* mine,' I said and that shut her up. For some reason my heart started pounding. Mama just stood for a moment looking out towards the ridge.

'Well is that so?' she said at last. 'And how many other people are in line to say that?'

'*What*? You talk about Harper that way? *Fuck* that. It ain't like that.'

She turned on me, spitting her words. 'How do you *know* that?'

I put my hand over my mouth, swallowed everything and breathed deep. 'Because I do,' I said. 'I just do.'

What I couldn't bring myself to tell her was that it didn't matter to me anyhow. I would have Harper any way I could. Being around her was the only thing I needed. It didn't matter that she'd taken the long route to get here. She was here now.

'She's using you like a life raft.'

'I don't care if she is,' I said, and I meant it. 'I love her.'

Mama's look softened. 'I know you do, honey, I know. But I don't want to see you making a terrible mistake, giving up your freedom, the chance of finding somebody who loves you back the way you deserve. Lord knows, I wasted some of *my* best years on somebody who didn't deserve it.'

'You think Harper don't deserve to be loved, Mama?'

'No, I do not think that, and you know it.'

We were both quiet for a long time. 'That baby needs a daddy.'

'I raised you on my own and we made out okay didn't we?'

'Sure we did,' I answered, automatic.

'You don't have to take on somebody else's responsibility...'

149

'Mama! Stop right there. All I need to know is that it *might* be my baby. As long as there's that chance, I'm here. I ain't *never* going to walk away from a woman carrying my child. I'm not that man, you hear me? That's not who I am.'

'No...' she said slowly and tears swelled in her eyes. 'But it's not your job to atone for his sins, John.'

That pissed me right off. 'This isn't anything to do with him! This is about me and Harper and me doing right by her.'

She hauled in a big breath. 'I am proud of that, of who you are, but there's something in you... I don't know... people can mistake it for a weakness and they'll take you for a ride and that's the truth.' She looked kind of defiant when she said it and all I wanted was deny it; it made me ashamed to hear her say it, like she thought I was just chicken shit, like Grady and them used to say.

I didn't know how to answer, so I stayed quiet, chewing on my thumbnail and staring out over the yard, thinking about Harper and the baby and where I might get me some more work. I started to walk away.

'Don't forget,' she raised her voice a little. 'It might more easily be Grady's baby. She has been living with him after all and he may have feelings just as strong as you do about that.'

Well, I lost it then. 'You don't think he *forfeited* any right to that by beating the *shit* out of her while she was carrying the child?'

'I know...' Mama closed her eyes for a moment and rubbed at her forehead. 'It's a terrible thing he did. Do you know what drove him to it? Did he...' she stopped. 'Don't look at me like that. I'm not excusing him his behaviour, but if she's been cheating on him and she knows he's got a temper...' she broke off.

'What? She only has herself to blame?'

'That is *not* what I meant, John. Don't you twist my meaning.'

150

But it sure as hell sounded like that's what she meant and I couldn't listen anymore.

'Okay, Mama, I think you've said enough,' I said, feeling old.

Harper'n me had made a plan to marry before the baby came. She didn't want me shut out of the delivery room when her time came, though Mama sured her that they wouldn't do that. I didn't mind her fear; I wanted to marry her. It felt as though she'd really be mine then and she'd finally believe I was hers. I told her I was the steadiest boy she'd ever know and nothing in the world would make me leave her, but well... Harper was Harper.

I remember the night well, now. Everything's peeled back and there it is raw and hurting, just waiting for me to look. To really look.

We'd just come out of the Walmart, late at night after a hard, hot summer rain. Harper could a done it all earlier in the daytime, Mama'd have took her, but Harper, she wanted us to get supplies together. So she waited until I finished my work at the paper mill. I remember pushing the cart alongside her and her excitement in the over cool of the air-conditioned aisles.

She had flip-flops with flowers on them, I remember, and her tight, full belly stuck out over her cut-off shorts. It was more than I could do to keep from stroking it all the time. Harper was excited, snapping gum as she talked, but every time she pitched something in the cart, she'd give me a look like she weren't so sure as she seemed.

'Put it in,' I'd tell her. 'You think we need it? Put it in.'

She'd say something about the money, but only for show; she knew I'd been earning good all summer and the paper mill was keeping me on.

She was a little way ahead of me when she stopped and something in the way she froze set every nerve in me off fizzing. Grady Epp was coming towards us from the far end and Harper, she looked like she lost every bit of colour she ever had. I reached out to her, I know I did, touched her on the arm and I remember how she shrugged me off before she said real low and scared, 'Don't tell him. Don't say anything, please.'

For a minute it looked as though he might just walk on by without saying nothing, but that wouldn't a been Grady so of course he stopped, so close he could have touched Harper right on the belly if he'd been minded to. He smelled of liquor.

I said his name and give him a nod before making to pass, my arm on Harper's back, but he angled himself so I'd have to butt him out of the way or stay right where I was.

'She got you running around doing errands for her? Cute,' he said and looked in the cart at all the new-born diapers, sleepsuits and the baby monitor we surely didn't need on account of the house being so small, but Harper had said she wanted to do it right.

So there's Grady standing there, filling up all the space like the quarterback he once was, and he's leering at Harper right in her face and my heart is pumping so hard and huge, it's like it's pulsing in my very eyeballs.

'Grady, let me get by,' she told him and I have to say I felt real proud of her the way she said it; strong, like she weren't going to take his shit and I knew for a fact she was scared to death of him. He reached out and stroked her jaw and I don't know how Harper felt about it, she was rigid as can be, but it sure bothered me.

'Harper,' he said and his voice was like he thought he was making love to her. 'When are you going to quit all this and come on home?' and I swear to god it seemed to me she was wavering, it truly did. And in that moment, I found my voice.

'Get your hands off my wife.'

Harper sucked her breath in, then hissed my name out.

'Your *what?*' Grady spun toward me like he was gon knock me out there and then, but somehow the fire in my belly the right on my side was bigger and I said, 'You heard me, asshole, Harper'n me we're married. Three days ago. Ain't nothing you can do about it.'

He was so mad I thought he was gon bust my jaw. He started spitting and yelling at her, at me. He grabbed my shirt and pushed me up against the cans of formula, hollering in my face.

'You lying, bastard, piece of shit! There's no way she'd hitch herself to a fuckin' faggot mama's boy piece of chicken shit like you! No way!' He was shaking me so hard and jerking my head against the shelves with his words.

Harper, she was screaming at him to stop. Then just as sudden as he started on me he stopped. We was both breathing and his face was so close to mine I could smell the liquor and tobacco, see the veins in his eyes, the yellowed edges. Security was coming up around the far side of the aisle and he clocked them right away, let go a me, took a step back and spat on the floor at my feet. Shaking his head at me, he said, 'You just don't get it, do you?'

After he'd gone, I held Harper while she raged and cried, and somebody brought her some water and told her to relax for the baby's sake. She was mad at me, mad at him, scared for the baby. And all the while I was telling her how sorry I was, I was thinking, but this was what you wanted. This is all you kep' on and on asking for me to do; stand up to him, be a man, *show* him.

Outside, the asphalt was steaming from the rain and Harper wouldn't talk to me. I left her with the cart and jogged through the puddles to my truck, pulled up close to her and got out to load everything we got for the baby. I let Harper be. She'd come around, I figured, but her silence was scorching.

To this day I don't know how he did it. One minute the place was deserted, the next he's got me in a arm-lock, gun pressed hard into my neck so hard I had trouble swallowing. Harper screamed and he shouted in my ear, 'Open your eyes, asshole!' pressing the gun harder. 'You keep them open and you *watch* what happens to people who dis*respect* me.'

It happened so fast. There was nothing I could have done, but it played out real slow whenever I closed my eyes for months after and I could always see things I could have, should have done.

I saw the terror in Harper's eyes, heard her beg him, for her sake, for the baby's sake, heard her tell him she'd leave me and come on home to him, just please don't hurt her. And then he shot her. And shot her. And shot her.

Grady's daddy blamed me for what happened. Propping up bars all around town he told his story of how I had made it my business to steal her away, humiliate his son in public, drove him to it. And Grady weren't around to say anything about that. He'd drove off that night on rain-slicked mountain roads, belly full of liquor, heart full of rage.

They found him the next day rammed into a tree. His daddy said he'd loved Harper and couldn't be without her. Only Mama came out and said it: that ain't what love looks like.

Things stand a little awkward between me and Reba over the next day or two. She shuts away around me; nice mannered but distant and talking mostly just to Sailor, who don't seem to be in any way weirded out by being in my van. I can't shake off the feeling of embarrassment at her taking me wrong over wanting to take her and Sailor away, nor the feeling of wishing they weren't there. Ain't nowhere for me to just be. It must be hard for her, though. No place to call her own, again.

'Do you think you could pick up my final pay packet from Levi?' she asks as I'm heading to work.

I tell her I will. 'We should talk, Reba. You need a plan. You can't stay hid away forever, it ain't good for the youngin.'

She gives me one a them looks that makes me want to suck my words back.

'I don't need anyone to tell me what good parenting is,' she snaps. Then right away tells me she's sorry. 'I think I have cabin fever.'

We both laugh a little.

I arrive late at Levi's and he's red in the face for having to work the bar for me. Folks are already shifting chairs and tables, turning them to face the raised platform at the far end of the bar room. I see Belle take her place. Her speaking voice is low. She can make it sound like you're in a dream.

'Well…' She draws out the word like she's pulling candy and looks about, slowly, smiling. 'Welcome… welcome. All of you.' There's a whistle from the crowd. 'E*specially* you, honey,' she says. 'Whoever you are!'

There's a scatter of clapping.

'Now, you all know the rules, folks!' She's standing by the rocker, facing out toward the bar room, packed tight with maybe eighty people, almost all known to me at least by sight. Belle, she always gets herself up good on Porch Lies night and tonight's no different. She has her hair piled up on her head, swirled like an ice cream cone and her wrists are jangling with silver and charms. I see she wears a fishing fly of Beau's in her ear, the blue of a jay-bird's feather catching at the light.

'No notes,' she tells us. 'No cheat sheets! Your story...' now everybody joins in like they always do, chanting along with her, 'True! *As remembered by you*!'

My heart trips. I been here a year or so now and I hadn't barely missed a one of these storytelling nights, so how is it I never heard until now, the significance of Belle's words?

There ain't nothing new in what she's saying. She opens this way every time; ribbing and corralling all the folks who love a story, reminding them of how it goes and then... and then, True, she says. *As remembered by you*. What is that? The truth is the truth. Right?

'Hey Belle!' someone hollers at her. 'When are *you* going to tell us a story?'

There's a friendly roar, more laughs and some oh yeahs and Belle swats at everybody like they ain't nothing but a bug that came in through the window.

'First up tonight, inspired by our seasonal Thanksgiving theme of homecoming, I expect you all to give a warm *welcome* home to a young lady who vowed never to return...'

'*Whoooh*...' a Mexican wave of voices swells across from one side the bar to the other as Belle starts to introduce the first yarn-spinner, but before she can go on, the street door slams open and in struts Brooke Adler. The two camera guys are with her and right off, the sound and good feeling in the room drops; it's like the bubbles in your soda gone flat. I hear someone say something about she better not be filming and a murmur of agreement.

It looks to me as though Brooke falters, surprised she don't get her usual hero's welcome. But she covers quick and while she settles at the bar with the two guys, folks loosen up again, laughing and shouting out for drinks and what not and so it takes me a minute to notice that Reba is there. Out of nowhere, there she is. She is right up close to Brooke, her head thrusting forward, finger jabbing and she is in a spitting fury.

'Take it outside!' someone shouts, and some folks laugh and look back to Belle, wanting her to go on and some look real interested and keep watching Brooke and Reba like it's a show they chose. But Reba, she ain't laughing and it looks like she don't even know anybody else is there.

'Well, now,' Beau murmurs under his hat.

I leave my place in the corner by the mirror and get out from behind the bar. Brooke catches my eye and looks a mix of relieved and pissed off.

'You fucking hypocritical piece of *trash!*' Reba's words come out fast, like she's put a slick of grease on her tongue to help em on their way. 'All that self-righteous crap you spout on your show, but these are real people's lives you're messing with, this is *my* life, my little boy's life,' she turns and points a finger at me. '*His* life. And for what?' She breaks off, draws breath. Reba's face is screwed up, ugly with fear and fury. 'Do you realise the danger you've put me and my child in?'

Folks in the bar are turning to look; some ain't never heard a word from Reba and they're liking the show. Others are real uncomfortable and Belle is stepping forward to take charge. She halts for a moment as Reba goes on.

'You couldn't have done a better job of leading my sister's killer to me and my little boy if you'd led him to us by the nose with a bull ring! You stupid, *stupid* piece of *trash!*'

Brooke Adler is protesting, reaching out a hand, but Reba ain't having it. She raises her head in that way I seen before; proud and fuck you. It's a look so strong, it silences Brooke Adler completely.

'You've robbed us. We were beginning to feel safe and you stole it. Shame on you, Brooke Adler.' She turns on her heel and she's gone, just like that.

Brooke looks a little shook up and before I realise it I'm asking her if she's okay.

'I guess so,' she says. 'But I'll be a lot better after a double rum and Coke.'

I'm torn with wanting to go after Reba and feeling the pointlessness of it, and while I'm paralysed with not knowing what to do, Belle makes an announcement.

'People,' she says in a loud, I mean business voice. 'I'm going to suggest a postponement of tonight's Porch Lies.' A loud groan swells through the crowd. 'Until I have a clear undertaking from the KYTV crew among us that they will respect the spirit of our community endeavour.'

Everybody quiets down until the whole bar is silent except for a few diehards in the backroom playing pool and foosball. Brooke Adler's soundman raises his hands like he's just along for the ride, but she shows surprise and looks about her with a look like she's wondering where all her buddies gone. I'm wondering the same thing, truth told. Only last week seemed she had just about everybody eating out of her hand.

Belle—man I admire that woman's heart—she just keeps her gaze on Brooke, level, calm and almost impossible to read. She ain't looking for a fight, or to look like the hot shot in front of all these people, she's just looking out for them is what she's doing; her people, her place.

Brooke raises her head and says, 'Please don't do that.' And before Belle can explain herself more clearly, Brooke Adler says, 'I'd like to share a story of my own.'

Belle looks genuinely taken aback and after being lost for words for a time, hurries to assure her, graciously, that everyone is welcome here.

'Well played, Brooke,' I say and she gives me a look says she has no idea what I could possibly mean.

Up in front of everybody, she seems small and I ain't never seen Brooke Adler as small. She takes a couple steps toward the mic and brushes at her hair, that's falling across her face. When she opens her mouth to talk, nothing comes out. Why that pisses me off, I don't know, but I sure hope she gets it together soon, she's making me uncomfortable.

She clears her throat, laughs and looks over towards Belle like she's sorry. Belle just nods and smiles at her, like she's got her back.

'To everyone who knew us, we were the perfect family,' she begins, and I think to myself, of course you were.

'It was your classic family set up. Mom, Dad, me and my younger brother. And yes... we had a dog...' she lets the laughter quiet down before she goes on. 'Dad worked for the sheriff's department, Mom was a homemaker. I think, for a time, we were okay, although looking back now there was probably always stuff going on that I was too young or too dumb to notice. My mom was quite a nervous woman. Anxious to please, over-reacted to any little mishap or mistake she made. But even so, every now and then when I was still in elementary school she'd suggest that she take a little part time job; to help out, to give her something outside the home and each time, Dad would veto it.

'In the early days he was smiles. Firm and very persuasive, but smiles. Later I came to recognise that the shine in his eye wasn't humour. Dad's reasons never changed, but they became more emphatic, because she wouldn't listen, he said. He wasn't having folks say he couldn't take care of his own family. Mom had more than enough to do taking care of the home, he said, and anyhow how did she think she'd manage a job when she could hardly keep things together at home? He hadn't liked to say anything, he said, but he was ashamed, yes *ashamed*: of her, of his home. She was getting real sloppy, he said. Lazy even. Taking everything for granted and letting things slide. I remember hearing him say this and the hit of shame *I* felt, without understanding why. I made a mental note to check my own attitude, to examine my own behaviour for sloppiness, or worse. I became super-vigilant and not just of myself.'

She takes a sip from a water glass and steps back up to the mic. 'Each time my father got mad at her, my mother promised to do better. She'd agree with him about how hard he worked and tell him how sorry she was that he couldn't even count on a nice homecoming. But things just got worse. She became more and more inept at the basic things she had to do to contribute to the smooth running of a family. There was always some way she was slipping up, or forgetting what he wanted.

'When I was around nine years old, my dad told me that if I didn't keep close tabs on my mother while he was out of the house and make sure she wasn't wasting time making calls or watching TV, in all likelihood my brother and I would get taken into care. You need to tell me, he said, what she does when I'm not here. Otherwise this whole family is going to be split up—sometimes he'd get real tearful telling me this—and you don't want to be responsible for that, do you? he'd ask. Your mother needs help, he'd say, I don't know what's wrong with her, but things are just about going to fall to pieces unless somebody makes sure she's keeping on top of the chores while I'm out of the house. I remember how important and proud I felt that my father trusted me, that he needed me.'

I realise that I'm listening real close to all this now, trying to see where it's going.

'I did as my dad asked, watched my mom's every move, corrected her when he wasn't around to do it and did my best to help. I studied hard, tried to keep my brother quiet when Dad was home. I did everything in my power to ward off the looming fear of disappointing and hurting my father. I wanted to make him proud of me, to make him happy. I wanted to be like him: hard working, righteous, strong. I had a horror that if I didn't guard against it day and night, I'd end up like my mother: weak, meek and useless at even the most basic of tasks.

'Despite my best efforts, however, we never could get it right. It was too hard.' She shakes her head. 'Every time he lost it, it broke another little piece of my heart. I adored my father, but he never could seem to believe it. And looking around, as he kept yelling at us to do, I could see he was right. I felt sorry for him coming home from a hard day at work keeping everybody safe, to a miserable, drab woman who couldn't even manage to keep the house clean. I felt sorry that he had to eat her dull, repetitive meals, when everybody else's wives made an effort.

'I started to resent my mother more and more for what she was putting us all through. She was the one making our lives so miserable. It was she who drove him to lose his temper, I could see it so clearly when Dad pointed it out. And by pointing out her faults, he was trying to help her improve, he said. He did it because he loved her and loved the family. If he didn't why would he take the trouble?'

'I'm ashamed to say that it was a long time after I'd left home, that the truth hit me. It probably hit *you* all about two minutes into my story, right?' she gives a laugh at her own expense and the room ripples with folks joining in, relieved that she's got it.

'My father,' she puts back her shoulders and her voice comes right out across the whole bar. 'My father was a cruel and controlling bully who spent the majority of his married life terrorising my mother. But you know what makes it so much worse? What makes it worse, is that I had been his accomplice.'

The room sighs, some folks gasp and even start to say it ain't so. She bows her head and raises her hands in a move that makes everybody still. She sure is good.

'Kids who grow up in households like mine are often left with a terrible legacy that can impact for the rest of their lives.' Someone gives that an amen and Brooke Adler

161

smiles in their direction. 'They can develop hyper-vigilance —like they're on a kind of permanent fight or flight mode —which can create intense anxiety, aggression or depression; sometimes all three. They develop eating disorders, drop out of high-school, suffer with poor self-esteem, display sexual promiscuity or recklessness. They frequently become drug or alcohol users who, if they work at all, move from one burger-flipping job to another. Alternatively, they can be driven by perfectionism and a need for over-achievement.

'I won't bore you with which boxes, if any, I ticked along the way, but I will say that my drive to succeed led me to be the first person in my family to go to college.

'Even then I credited my dad with this and went away for my freshman year determined never to turn out like my mother; drab dull, no interests, no achievements.

'Then, as often happens in all the best stories...' She waits for the laugh. It comes and she talks on. 'fate took a hand and I had a chance meeting in my first semester of college. A substitute teacher came up to me after class and asked if I was Cora-Lynn's girl. I was surprised. My mother had few friends. I said that I was and this smart, peppy woman just about melted in front of my eyes. "Your mother and I were in high school together!" she told me and went on to paint a picture of a sassy, popular, super-bright young woman who had dreams and drive and ambition.

'"So, did she do it? Did she make Principle? She always wanted to teach high-school and work her way up."

'I was speechless. I literally couldn't say a word. How could I? What could I say? That my mother was a meagre, dull little woman of whom I was ashamed? She carried on talking, evidently unaware of my discomfort. She told me she'd known who I was the moment she set eyes on me. Well, that just about slayed me, but it was about to get worse.'

She takes a big breath while everybody in the room seems like to hold theirs.

'Yeah,' she says, looking slowly round the room. 'Some of you are there already. You know what's coming, right?' There's a short murmur of laughter and she smiles a little before going on. 'She told me—and these are her words, exactly as I remember them—she told me, you are just exactly like she was at your age.'

She don't say nothing for a time. She's playing it so good I almost feel sorry for her. She takes up her story once more. 'I wish I could say,' she tells the room, 'that there and then I resolved to do right by my mother. That would make a pretty story, right? But in truth, it took me a while to let any of this sink in.

'Fast forward to my first job as a rookie reporter.' Her voice is changed. She's made it more upbeat, go getting. 'I was excited to get my first job out of college, working for the Mountain Herald.'

My skin prickles. She looks over in my direction once again, but she's too far and the light's all wrong for me to see what's in her eyes.

'A few months in, I was sent to cover a story that changed my life.' I blow out a breath and the heat in me rises. 'A 23-year-old girl by the name of Harper Eyman, heavily pregnant with her first child, was shot and killed by her former partner. It was my job to cover this story, to write compelling copy and inform our readers. And who better to shine a light on the unseen side of these sorts of stories, than me? I'd lived it first-hand, right? Maybe not to such extremes, but I knew personally how much misunderstanding there was around these sorts of issues. I filed my copy under the headline, Two Sides to Every Story.

'Now make no mistake, I never said nor believed that what Grady Epp did wasn't terribly, terribly wrong, but I wanted to show how a man might be driven to it. And just as soon as I started talking to people who knew her, it was

163

obvious to me that this deeply troubled young woman had disrespected and provoked her ex-partner to the point of unbearable pain and despair. As I saw it, she was as much to blame as he was. She had got bored with him and moved on, as was her pattern, to another man despite already being pregnant and the two of them had taunted him and cruelly flaunted their relationship around town for everyone to see.'

She's stopped talking and the whole room is silent, but I ain't sure if I'd hear her start up again cause the blood is roaring in my ears. There's something in her look, her body that's like a challenge, like she's daring someone, anyone to call her out. My throat is choked up and burning dry and chilled pins and needles shoot up the back of my neck and over my scalp. I want to do something to stop her. I don't understand what she's doing, why she's telling this story like it's hers. I want to stop her from dragging a dead girl through the mud who can't talk no more and never found a way to holler loud enough so's anybody paid her any mind.

I hate myself for my cowardice and see it has always been there. I ask myself would it make any difference to Harper if I got up and told the truth? Would anyone believe me? What stops me? What?

She's taken up talking again and I keep still for now, until I feel a shock of stinging pain in the palm of my hand and realise the glass I been holding in my hand has broke. I stare at it before putting it under the cold tap and watch the blood sluice into the sink. I don't care if Levi sees me.

'It took another chance meeting before I realised what a terrible, terrible lie I had been living. And as of now, standing here in front of you all, I can tell you that I haven't forgiven myself. I don't know if I ever will. For the hurt and pain I caused, for the dangerous myths I willingly peddled, and for betraying my mother.' Her voice cracks and she takes another drink. 'So, what changed?'

Now she's got the whole room hanging on her every word, myself included. She's swerved a corner I weren't expecting.

'I saw an interview with a remarkable woman who had set up the Tennessee Women's co-operative and shelter and to cut a long story short, I went to meet her and the volunteers to see for myself. I finally learned that I had been a victim too. I came to understand that you can behave as badly as you like, not do your chores, go out and get a job, refuse a second date, whatever... you can be a pain in the ass! But it is never an excuse for ridiculing, tormenting, belittling, controlling, humiliating, punishing...' she breaks off and she's red-faced, breathing hard. She pulls herself together and finishes, her voice trembling and cracking on the words. 'It is never an excuse.'

She rakes her hand through her hair and I can see she's shaking. Someone hands her a glass of water, which she takes and drains.

'It was too late to tell my mother, to ask her forgiveness, to let her know that it was not her fault, that he was a hateful, vicious bully. But it's not too late to try and give her a voice, through my work and the stories I cover while at the same time, facing up to my responsibilities.'

Someone whoops, 'Yeah!'

'Thank you for listening.' She smiles. 'But before I sign off, for what it's worth, I want to offer something up. What I've learned is, running from the pain we feel or that we caused is never going to work. It will always catch you up and outrun you, so...'

There's a hush for a minute, then Belle begins to clap. She's joined by some others until they're all clapping and there's a couple yelps and a whistle and she's surrounded by people hugging her and helping her over to her crew at the far end of the bar. I can hear the voices of people I know and those I don't, chewing on the whole thing, saying how brave she is, how clever the way she set herself up to be hated, what a kick-ass story teller, the way she made you think one thing and suddenly, blah, fuckin, blah, and hasn't she made her mama proud anyhow and on and on…

But me, I'm not clapping, I'm not breathing. All I'm doing is thinking fuck you. Fuck you. Fuck. You.

And before I know it I'm hollering across the whole stinking bar, '*Fuck you Brooke Adler! That ain't you your story to tell! Fuck you!*'

Then I'm caught in the headlights of Lark's look. She's shocked, I can see, by my hollering at Brooke and I can't face her or anybody. I toss my dishtowel down, don't even think to take off my apron, and I head out. Levi's sure to fire me this time.

It's cold and there's a high moon, far off and lonely. When I finally cool off from my anger, I find myself remembering how Mama always used to tell me to watch for them that's quick and hot about a thing. 'It can give you insight.'

I didn't know what the word meant and on asking her, she did what she always did.

'Work it out,' she said. 'Think about it. Break the word down. What might it mean?' and forever after I saw it as a word meaning to get inside, right inside a person. But it's only now I'm thinking that when she told me to pay attention to what a person gets riled up about, she didn't just mean other folks; she was telling me to look inside myself too. Only it's too late now. What's the use in seeing it now? Past is past. Done. For better for worse and not any amount of hoeing it over and looking for clues is like to change what happened. If I thought it might, I'd tear myself open right now.

I start to shiver bad, and realise I left my jacket behind when I ran out. I make my way back, hoping to avoid any eyes and faces, but as I sneak through the kitchen fire exit I stop dead in my tracks. I cannot take in what I'm seeing.

166

Lark is standing by the coat hooks, my jacket at her feet, just like as though she dropped it and she looks up from what she's holding as I come in. Her eyes are huge. Her face flushed and blotchy.

She's holding my little wooden box in her two hands, real gentle, running one of them over its top like she's soothing it. I pull at my collar and blow out but I can't seem to pull any air back in and my head's feeling cold and light, my hands all pins and needles, no feeling.

I want to reach out and touch it, feel the smooth wood, trace the dents and scratches it's taken on from being carried around more than a year with no resting place. My chest feels tight. I want to pick it up and hold it, remind myself of how it feels, but now it's sitting out there, exposed in the light, I find I can't.

'Why, Lark?' I ask her, and I don't even know exactly what I'm asking her.

'Brooke...' she trails off and I'm glad of her shame; she's Lark. 'It's yours?'

'I believe it is,' I tell her and colour up hot and she makes a noise; a sucking sound like she's dragging hard on a cigarette.

I want to take my things and leave but I feel awkward, not sure if I should say anything, explain myself why I have a baby's urn in my possession.

At last I let myself reach out and touch it, running my fingers across the top. I take it from her and sit it on the palm of my hand and read it, though I don't need to, to know what it says: John Eyman McArthur July 10th 2009-July 16th 2009

'They said it weren't mine to take.'

Lark seems surprised to hear my voice and I can't say I blame her; we been walking for close on half an hour and I ain't said a word.

'But you thought it was?'

I put my hand on the small bulky shape in my pocket and nod. But I'm trying to remember what it was that I had thought. I don't remember thinking much of anything by then. Now I can't stop and it's bad.

'Do you want to talk about it, Cassidy?'

I fight a powerful urge to do it; to open up and tell her, get it off my chest and make it stop pushing and pushing and *pushing* at me.

More and more over the past few weeks it's felt like I have a lump of something hard and twisted, wedged inside my throat and I want it out. I want it out.

I sneak me a look at her face. She catches it right away and smiles like she knows everything's gon be okay. But I'm thinking about how her face would change if I told her everything.

'It's fine,' I say. 'It can stay where it is.'

'What do you mean?'

'It's done. Talking about it won't change anything.'

'Well now that's where you're wrong! Everybody knows it's good to talk and...' she breaks off a minute, and claps her hand over her mouth, pressing it hard. She tries to speak. 'Surely sharing—oh God,' she sounds raw. 'It was a baby.' She almost sobs the word out. 'Whose was it? What happened to that baby?'

She puts a hand on my arm and even though I know she means well, I won't allow it.

'What are you saying?' I ask her, and I sound ugly. 'You saying I just need to share my story and I'll be absolved? It'll all be okay and none of it would of happened?'

'Of course not! All I'm saying is...'

'It's too late, Lark. What happened, happened. Ain't no use hauling it out now. Past is past. Not any amount of raking it over is gon change that.'

'I wasn't saying that.' She's stopped walking. 'But you're carrying something terrible around with you and...'

168

'I don't need your help,' I tell her, as rough as I can without yelling. 'I don't need you sneaking in my things because Brooke Adler tells you to.' Her face flushes and as she turns her head, her eyes fill with tears. 'You know what, Lark? I specially don't need help from the very person who *started* this shit storm.'

She takes a step back and looks at me, white faced.

'What do you mean?' her voice is shaky.

'You need me to spell it out? Okay. Brooke Adler told me that it was you called the TV station and told her where to find Reba. Uh huh! Right there! You and her in cahoots right from the start.'

'What do you mean 'right there'? That wasn't me!'

I start walking and try and shut out her voice as she calls out, 'I never called her! Cassidy! Stop!' she catches up with me and she is so mad I stop.

'You know what, Cassidy, or John, or whatever the hell your name is, you need to step up! Step up! Brooke Adler can only take what you let her take.

'Sometimes you've just got to roll your sleeves up. How do you want to look back on yourself a year from now? Five? Ten? Someone who never took another risk? Still hiding out from life?'

And I think, no, I don't want that to be it, but I don't know how to change it.

We walk back together in silence. When we get to Levi's, she says, 'I'm sorry I went in your things. She said you had a gun and I was scared for you. I thought...'

She doesn't finish, and I wonder who she was scared for. 'I never had a gun, Lark. I never will.'

'I thought you might hurt yourself,' she says, and her voice chokes itself off.

I pull her into a hug then and tell her I'm sorry.

'I'm sorry I frightened you,' I tell her and I run one of my hands up the back of her neck, holding her against me and massaging the soft, short, buzzed hair with the pads of my fingers.

Inside, the last person has told their story and folks are talking the night over, enjoying a drink and flying and bumping up against Brooke Adler like they're moths and she's the flame. She looks up and catches my eye and we look at each other for a long moment. And I think of how she talked and how she told it like she saw it, and I think, you don't get to decide. You don't get to decide what I'm guilty of.

I ain't never been one for showmanship, folks all around me been doing a good enough job of that along with the ghost of my daddy, for as long as I can remember. But right about now it seems to me there's only one thing I can do. I am done with other people telling my story. It's over.

I walk around the bar and reach underneath the counter. I look about for Lark and when I catch her eye, without taking my eyes from her, I flip the switch. Power goes off, like that. Juke box whines and halts, TV shuts off and it's darkness, excepting the candle light over by Belle's Thanksgiving arrangement. It feels like an age, but most likely it's seconds before the room's in uproar. Folks are calling out, some uneasy, some laughing. A voice shouts, 'I thought this was Thanksgiving, we already had Halloween!' There's whoops and hollers and a lot a laughter and some nervous talk.

I make my way towards the light.

I get in front of the mic, in front of all them people; them that know me, them that don't. Over by the back of the bar, in the low light, I see these people, truly see them; these people who come in here week on week, sharing themselves, leaning on each other, helping and hurting.

I can just about make out Freak, who disappears every now and again when he can't shake off the blues and Mattie Larson, who lost all three of her kids to social care, one by one. And right there's Ev's cousin, who done time in juvenile hall for a hit and run when she weren't but fifteen years old. I get to feeling that maybe I'm in good company.

'Hey, everybody,' I begin and it's just a rasp. I clear my throat and breathe deep. I see Beau, over in his usual spot, nod his head at me.

'I guess I'm about ready to tell my story.' I can feel how my voice cracks and trembles more than hear it and I can't say nothing else, can barely move.

'*Well get on with it, then!*' Somebody calls out. Voices hush him, the room stretches and shifts.

Beau runs his bow across the strings of his fiddle, making it sing a little and the tension eases.

'What is it Belle always tells us?' I shoot a look at her and she nods and smiles at me. 'That stories are how we make sense of ourselves? To see where and how we fit? Something like that anyhow.' I stop again and my throat is dry.

The whole room is willing me please god to say something. I look at Lark again and she holds my gaze and just when I think all I can do is quit, her mouth flickers and I can see the ghost of her smile.

'My name,' I say it loud, surprising myself and a few others besides. 'Is John Cassidy McArthur. Some folks know me as John C. You all know me by Cassidy, but it's all the same. I am who I am.' I breathe in again and see Lark sit straighter and smile at me a little. I can't look at her for long, I want to keep it together and there's something in her expression that undoes me.

'The truth of the matter is that by now, most of you all know me as a thief, a drunk and a coward; and you know it from Brooke Adler.

'Working like I do,' I say, wandering blind, for the moment, through my thoughts. 'I seen that everybody goes through hard times. Makes mistakes or bad decisions. You get through it, given time maybe. Maybe not. When I first

171

come here, I been on the road for a long time, moving on from one place to another. And I would a moved on for sure if I hadn't been snowed in.' I smile a little; some of them laugh. 'By the time a thaw came and I might ha' moved on, you all had got a little under my skin, I guess. And so I stayed.' I peer out into the room and my mouth is so dry I can hardly ask for a glass a water. I don't see who it is hands me one, but I take it and drink.

'Belle says just tell the truth as you remember it. So that's what I'm minded to do, because I been robbed.' I look over to where Brooke Adler and her KYTV crew are. 'But I done it to myself too. So, here it is. The truth as I remember it.'

I look up for a minute. In my heart I know Harper, she'd be laughing at me and it makes me smile.

'When I was a boy about so high,' I put my hand against my thigh. 'My mama and me, we moved to Mason from someplace she always said didn't even have a gas station. We settled in, but there'd weren't a week went by without somebody or other reminding us we weren't from around here. So, when Harper came from who only knew where, to live with her grandma, Lucille, we was right away like two little nuthatches, always together. Folks used to get on my case about me being so friendly with a girl, always telling mama in my hearing that I was for sure gon turn out weird if she didn't get some men in my life. Mostly she'd smile and give them the finger when their back was turned and tell me she was tryin' to *avoid* any men in my life. All the men she knew spent their time drinking and beating up on folks, usually women and youngins. She'd tell me I was different, gentle, and she didn't want me getting influenced by any no-good men. I'd feel real uncomfortable when she said it.

'Harper'n me, we was inseparable friends until she started running with Grady Epp and his crowd; after that she hardly gave me a look; they were more fun than I was, she said, they was livin' life and she wanted some. Eve'body in town knew he was rough, but he was liked as well and folks enjoyed him; he could start a party in a morgue, if he was in mind to. But you know... he could start a fight in an empty house just as easy.

'Every time I think about what made me do different for once, I come up empty.' I stop then, because that's a lie. Or rather it was true once, but not anymore.

'This is hard,' I say. Now the flood of righteousness rushing through me has subsided a little, I ain't got so much to drive on.

'You know what?' I look out at nobody in particular, but I'm picturing Lark. 'I ain't comin' up empty no more. I know why I broke the habit of my lifetime and spoke up in that parking lot. I wish I could say I did it on account of it being the right thing to do. That staying silent like always was cowardly. But it was swell-headed pride that drove me. And spite. I had something Grady didn't never have; Harper's promise, and I wanted him to know it and believe it and feel it and *hurt*. Oh man, how I wanted him to hurt.

'I had a belly full of mock and jeer my whole life from him. And Harper, she gave me her fair share too, tellin' me I warn't doing right by her, not standin' up for her nor myself. And eve'time I get to thinkin' like that, I know I ain't no better'n Grady and his Daddy, and all a them folks calling out judgment on Harper and sayin' she drove him to it.

'But anyhow, like I say, if I was telling my story like I wished it was—wished *I* was—we'd all come out a whole lot different to how we all *really* was.'

I look around the room and think. I remember how many times preacher would say something about anybody without sin could cast the first stone and folks would leave church and go on out into the sunlight carrying them words in his heart for about the time it takes to get home, then carry on same as ever, casting stones, casting stones.

173

'When Brooke Adler's story first broke on TV, it didn't touch me. Not in the way some might expect. Reason why, is I had already taken everything on. She weren't tellin' me nothin' I didn't already think of myself; Harper was killed on account of me, my baby son was killed on account of me, my little brother Petey...' I can't finish my sentence for a minute and have the strongest sensation of if I try and make any sound, I will crack into pieces. I put my head back, breathe in, blow out and try again. 'Well, let's just say for now some things have changed, but I will always be responsible for what happened to Petey.

'Harper and me, we'd been married three days when Grady shot her in the parking lot of the Wal Mart. I still don't remember much detail—one a the nurses said most likely I had a trauma—but some things is seared on my brain for always. It seemed to take forever until emergency services got to us. I was scared to death and trying so hard to do the right thing. There was so many holes in her, so much blood... I didn't know where to put my hands first. I remember thinking if I could just plug the holes, she'd be... I could keep her... I just needed to stop the life pouring out of her. I had my shirt off, tried to use that, somebody runnin' out from the store, tore open the package of new-born diapers and used one to try and stop the flow, but it just kept comin'.' I stop again, remembering the way her blood, Harper's blood, rose up between my fingers.

My throat hurts, my nose stings. I think about how Brooke Adler reported Lucille telling her how I stood by and did nothing, just cried like a baby. Well Lucille, she weren't there, of course, but she was right about me crying like a baby. I guess she thought she knew me.

'Harper was pronounced dead on arrival and all the attention turned to saving that baby. I didn't never understand until then what it meant to *will* something to happen. It's so powerful, you can convince yourself it will

174

come to pass. Doctors was doin' what they do and I was willin' that baby to hold on and pull through. So much so that every muscle and bone in my body was wired and tight and springin' with it. That baby was gon live and I was gon make it up to him, best I could.

'For six days, he held on. Man what a fighter. Every day we was told to prepare ourselves and every day came and went. Lucille came and went too and it was like I was a ghost in the room; she looked straight through me, never spoke a word to me; not of comfort nor accusation; never asked what had happened. On the sixth day, she kicked the chair I was sitting on, woke me up—I couldn't help but sleep, though I swore I wouldn't—and I saw in her face right away. It was all over. There's a strange and terrible feeling of relief in that, but it don't last.

'I could tell you about the cryin' and grievin', about the funerals and the loneliness and isolation. I could tell you about how I blamed myself and blamed myself and wanted somebody to tell me it was okay. But nobody did. And they were right; it weren't.

'It must have been four or five weeks after that I got a call at the house from the funeral home tellin me that Lucille had called to say she was coming to take John junior's ashes and they wanted to check with me. Well I told em no, that weren't right and I'd be right on by and get em myself.'

I pause and take a breath. 'Maybe now's the time to let y'all know that I hadn't been sober then for weeks. I started as soon as I woke and kept it up until I passed out for sleep. And that's how I was when I got behind the wheel of my truck and somehow made it th'eight miles to the funeral home. But Lucille, she beat me to it and knowing eve'body in town like she did, talked him into letting her take the ashes. Well after all, he said when I made it to the funeral home, she was the baby's close kin too and ain't I stayed away all this time despite all their calls? I remember how he

175

took a couple steps back from me and the look on his face showed me what all he thought of me turning up there unwashed and drunk in the middle of the day. He knew he done the right thing.

'I can't recall ever feeling like I felt then. Like some kind of animal, crazy with wanting to destroy something, anything, everything. I wanted to howl and roar and I remember driving again, fast, and you can be sure I thank the lord daily, that I didn't kill nobody on the road that day by my drivin…

'I don't remember much after that but waking up the next morning still in my clothes, sick to my stomach, with a terrible smell of burning rubber coming to me through the open window. That and the sounds of sirens.

'Outside, the sun was already hot in the sky and my head hurt so bad I couldn't hardly open my eyes. My mind was filled with black and I didn't see Mama come at me, but next thing I know, she's scratching my face, beating on me, her words comin' out like she's possessed. I can't forget how it sounded; raw, sliced right open. *Why wasn't it you? It should have been you.* And how could I disagree with that?

'It seems that not only had I left my truck unlocked when I, by some miracle, made it home from wherever in hell I'd been, I had also forgot to put the handbrake on. I broke the first rule of living in the mountains. Always leave your vehicle in gear; put on the handbrake. You grow up learning that alongside The Lord's Prayer and how to bait a hook with a piece a bread. Part of our DNA, I been told. So you see, when my little brother, this sweet little guy, who never judged me nor grudged me nothin', who had a heart full of sunshine, when he climbed into my unlocked truck to play at firefighters, it didn't take but a few minutes before he'd knocked it out of gear and it started to roll backwards. He must have been so scared. Maybe he called out for me, or mama. But no one came and the truck just kept on rolling, back down the drive, across the narrow road until

176

there weren't no road left, just the edge of the gorge and the trees that broke it's fall, but not enough.'

And so, it's over and I'm done and there's silence and static and me, I feel tears washing, endless over my face. And I'm tired and a little piece empty.

Somehow, I make it out to the parking lot, a strong need for air and some space hitting me out of nowhere. I lean my back against the dumpster and wait for the beat of my heart to slow and the heat in my face to cool a little. I can hear voices coming through the muffle of the fire door and clapping and I want to get as far away as possible, but I got no strength in my legs just now.

Just when I think I can start the walk home, I get a yank of tired frustration as the fire exit screeches and thumps open and I see Lark.

She don't say nothing, just comes alongside me and sighs deep.

'Hey, Lark,' I say, wishing she'd leave me be, wanting her to stay. I want to ask if she was there all along, but I'm scared that she was and scared that she wasn't and it don't matter anyhow because right away she says, 'I heard your story.'

I nod.

'I thought it was really brave. That must have been the hardest thing to do.'

I shrug, 'I ain't brave, Lark. I'm just tired.'

She leans closer, just enough for me to feel the pressure and a bit of warmth, before she straightens up again.

'What made you do it? After all this time? So... so publicly?'

I look at her sharp. 'What do you mean?'

Her voice comes soothing. 'Well, it just seems so out of character. You... you're such a private person, I can't imagine what you must have been feeling, to get up there like that.'

177

I think about it for a minute and start to wander in my head on the differences between private and secretive and which is it I am, and now I ain't got a secret will anything change at all or am I still gon be lonely the rest of my life like she once told me.

'I don't know. I weren't thinking.'

Lark sounds like she's holding a laugh inside her mouth. 'I wondered what you were feeling, not what you were thinking.'

I'm confused. I look her in the eye and it don't look like she's making fun of me, it looks like she trying to make sense of me.

We're halfway out of the parking lot, headed for my barn before I realise we're walking. I think about Brooke Adler shaping the world into something she can package. How she come tramping through my life, Reba's too, looking for a story to make her name, to make up for something or other I don't really understand.

'You saw it, Lark,' I say, just as if she were in my head with me, with all my tumbling thoughts. 'The way she took a story and made it what she wanted, twisting and tying it until she'd taken its soul. Each time I saw her face or heard her voice laying on the judgement, and inviting folks to give their verdict over and over again...' I break off for a time to find the words to explain something I can't explain and so I just say, 'Comes a time I guess when you realise you can't feel no worse than you already do. I hated myself already—Brooke Adler didn't point out anything I didn't already know, even if she wasn't in possession of all the facts. I guess I realised that all the folks in the world couldn't hate me and judge me more'n I did myself so... might as well go ahead and do it—tear off the band-aid. It was a piece of shit band aid anyhow...' she smiles along with me. 'And you know what? I hate a righteous person who got nothin' to be righteous about.'

'Well, whatever your reasons, surely it feels good to finally get it off your chest.'

'No, Lark,' I say feeling suddenly mad at her and her easy way. 'Nothin's changed, can't you see that? This ain't one a your stupid TV shows. I still killed my little brother. I was a chicken-shit-coward drunk and I killed him. Nothin's changed, my mama lost her baby because a me.' I can't seem to stop my voice rising. 'I can't bring him back... I can't...' and I can't speak no more when I'm gasping for breath and I feel Lark's arms about me and I shove at her to leave me be, but she stays right there by my side steady and quiet before she puts a hand on my arm again and I let her. I let her hold me while I sink to the ground and I cry and I cry and I cry for my mama and my brother and for Harper and yes I cry for me too.

It's some time before the clear, hard cold creeps up around me and I start to notice a little more outside of myself. We're sitting on the solid ground, backs against a big old tree a few minutes' walk from my barn. And small as she is, Lark's got me in her arms and she's rubbing at my head, slow and good like I'm some animal needs quieting. I can feel the pads of her fingers through my hair, rhythmic and steady. I sit up and put an arm around her, draw her close to me and kiss her head through her woollen hat. Thank-you.

It's a beautiful night, for all the cold. Sky's clear and full to as can be with drifting stars that put me in mind of them flocks of swallows just before dark.

'You have school tomorrow? You shouldn't have come all this way. Where's your car? I'll walk you back.'

'I could come in for a bit,' she says and right then I remember I got Reba and her youngin in there.

I feel uncomfortable and pull away from her which she takes for I don't know what, but she shuts right down.

'Forget it,' she says all stiff, like she has something to be shamed for. 'You don't need to walk me, Cassidy, I know my way.'

'Sure you do, Lark, but it don't feel right setting you off on your own. I'll come with you.'

I can tell she don't want me to and once again, the easy between us is gone and I want to haul it back and hold on to it, it felt so comfortable and good to me. 'Lark, I got someone staying, is all. Otherwise for sure I'd invite you in...'

'Someone staying?' she sounds as though I just told her we was living on the moon. 'You really are a dark horse. Is it someone from home?' My feeling of discomfort grows, and she picks up on it right away. 'It's none of my business, I'm sorry.'

And all at once I think, I'm done hiding, so I say. 'It's Reba and her youngin. They needed a place to stay and I wanted to help. I figured if it weren't for me...'

She quirks an eyebrow at me like she ain't buying it and says, her voice a little cooler. 'You don't need to explain yourself, you've always liked her, I'm sure she's grateful for your help.'

'What that supposed to mean?'

'Nothing, it's not supposed to mean anything. Just that you've always liked her, so it shouldn't be a surprise to me that you're helping her.'

'So, if it's not a surprise, Lark, what is it?' I ask, surprising myself and her too by the look on her face.

She stops and turns to face me, hands on her hips. 'What do you think, Cassidy?' she asks. She sounds mad, but I can't figure out why for sure. 'I've been making a fool of myself over you for so long, I would have thought even you, wrapped up in yourself as you are, would have realised by now.'

Her words sting. 'What? You're not a fool, Lark.'

'I am for you,' she says. 'And everybody but you sees it. And seeing as we seem to be having a night for truths, I may as well tell you.'

'Tell me what, Lark?' I don't know why I'm pushing her like this, but I can't seem to help myself. 'Why are you a fool? All you've ever been is good to me, and I know I didn't always make it easy. Maybe you're too good.'

Well that just lets the whole thing loose and now she's mad as hell.

'There's no such thing as being too good, you idiot! But there is such a thing as being too stupid to read the signs and let a thing go.' Her breath catches hard and she says, 'I'm in love with you, Cassidy,' sounding anything but loving, truth be told. 'Ever since I hauled your stupid ass out of a blizzard, I've had a thing for you, but you don't feel the same way and I don't think you ever will, and I need to just let it go. No, *don't*,' she says swatting me away as I start to tell her I do care for her. 'I know you care for me, Cassidy, but not the same way and I don't want to make you feel awkward.'

'I don't, you don't... oh, Lark... I'm sorry.' I mean I'm sorry that I'm such a pain in the ass, but she takes it as I'm sorry for not feeling the same way and somehow it gets more difficult.

'You don't owe me anything.'

'Lark, you been so good to me, if I took you for granted, I'm sorry, I really am. But Reba...' Lark butts right in, fast.

'I don't want to hear about you and Reba, I don't mean to be petty and I hope you two work it out, I really do, but I don't want to know...'

'Stop it, Lark!' It's my turn to butt in. 'There ain't nothing like that between us, but I ain't gon lie, I might have wanted it. It took me a little while before I saw it weren't her I wanted but... but, something about her. I

181

mean I really like her and all, but...' I stop then, frustrated again by words failing me, always failing me.

We walk in silence, feet ringing together until we get to Lark's car, alone and dark in the middle of the empty parking lot outside Levi's and I'm glad I kept her company.

'I ain't never been loved by an easy person, Lark.'

'What do you mean?'

'I don't know. I guess I mean, how would I know it when I see it? Don't be mad at me or feel a fool on account of my blindness.'

I want to tell her what I been too scared to let in for a long, long time; that she means the world to me; that I care about how she feels and how she's doing. I want to tell her that every damn time the door opens at Levi's, I'm looking to see if it's her and I'm low when it ain't and lifted right up when it is. I want to tell her that right now ain't the first time I've wanted to run my fingers in her hair and see how her mouth'd feel on mine. But I tell myself she won't hear me right and so the whole tangle of words get caught up in back of my throat and stay right where they are, unsaid. Lark looks small to me and sad and we hug for a long time before she gets in her car and drives off.

When I get back to my camper it's empty. I can see right away that Reba's gone. Place is tidier'n I ever kept it even though I ain't no slob, and there's a feeling of lonely. The smell of her is still in the air and I suck it in, knowing it'll be gone soon as well.

My money's gone too and a note and two twenty-dollar bills is weighted down on the counter by the empty jar.

Cassidy, you've been a real friend to me and I'll never forget that. Thank you for taking us in when I didn't know where to turn to. I've taken all your money except something for groceries, I'm sorry, so I owe you that too and you'll get it back I promise, one way or another if it's the last thing I do. Just don't go hiding out again so a body can't find you. I need to get away and back on track. I know you'll understand.

I hope you find what it is you're looking for Cassidy, but I have a feeling a lot of it is already all around you. You're a good man no matter what anybody says about you. I'll think of you always.

Have a life!

Love always, your friends Reba and Sailor.

I read it over three or four times then put it aside and look about me. It hits me hard that I most probably won't never see them again.

I lay for a long time in the dark, thinking about all what happened. It sure don't feel like it was only today I was stood up there in front of all them folks, spilling my guts. I think about how Lark seemed to think I should feel different afterwards. Why? Because all them TV shows she watches with Ev? Nah... Lark, she's smarter'n that. Maybe she knows something I don't. For sure I feel less scared, less tight with fear of more'n more stuff coming out. There is no more, I am emptied out. And then something comes to me and it makes me sit up.

I been walking with this feeling of bottomed-out empty so much of the time, that it's took me a while to notice something *has* changed. This feeling inside me, it's not empty: it's space; room to breathe.

I lay back down and let go my body and my bones and I got nothing on my mind but Lark; her face when she come out of the bar and found me; how she stayed with me, got close and listened to what I had to say. I don't know when it is exactly, I slide into sleep, but last thing I remember is that I ain't afraid to close my eyes.

3

It's around 7am, a good few months since Thanksgiving Porch Lies, and I'm out back of Beau's barn, tossing my wash bucket of water out over the grass. Straightening, I stop in my tracks at the sight of the prettiest sunrise I seen in years. Mist is rising from the fields, and there's a long band of silver light, streaking along the edge of the sky.

When I was a little boy, Mama used to take me out to the edges of the woods behind our home and listen out for spring sounds. She'd get me up early for school, put a finger over her lips to let me know we was gon do different to usual and out we'd go in our bare feet, with a pop tart or a piece a waffle and see what we could find. There'd be a smell in the air of damp earth and bark and a softness that'd been gone for so long it felt like it were gone forever.

I turn back, but the two-note trill and whistle of a tufted titmouse stops me and swear to god it almost makes me laugh out loud.

Something's tugging on me to keep out there in the light, listening to the birds having their morning meet and greet. I drag a blanket out and wrap it round me and I'm still sitting on a stump with my coffee and bowl of cold cereal when I see Lark coming across the field with her daddy's dog jumping over the place like he aint never been outside before.

Lark's excited and talking high pitched, but I can't make out what she's saying. I just keep smiling at her like the fool I am.

'Cassidy! I've found the most wonderful thing, come take a look!'

'Hey there, Lark.'

'What?' she stops her bubbling and looks at me closer.

'Nothin,' I say, but maybe she can tell she's making me smile. I squint into the sunshine to see if I can make out her expression a little.

'Did you just get up?' she asks, eyeing my blanket I guess.

'I been up for while,' I tell her. 'I heard me the first of spring this morning and I feel good.'

She smiles at me and tells me to come take a look at what she's brought along in her car, so we trail up together, me telling her about nuthatches and titmice and all, and how me and Mama used to listen for them.

She says, 'I feel like I'm witnessing you emerge from hibernation,' and she reaches over and ruffles my hair.

And I think about how me and Harper found a wood frog looked like he was dead, out in the woods when I was a kid. Harper told me their hearts stop and they get actual ice crystals in their blood until they come out into the spring again.

By the side of the road she opens her trunk and almost whoops, 'Look at this beauty!'

She's pulling a dust sheet off of something, though truth be told there is more dust under it than on it, and she sits on the tailgate, triumphant. I can see right away what it is, but she's talking again.

'Freak showed it to me, it needs work, but the minute I saw it I thought of you and your vinyl collection and I knew you had to have it.' She falters like an engine stuttering then starting again. She goes on a little uncertain now. 'You don't mind, do you?'

Mind? How can I tell her that the very idea of her thinking of me when I ain't even around makes me want to cry? She's lifted the lid and I can see it's a fine old turntable, suitcase style, coloured same mossy green as a flycatcher's belly and she's gone real quiet.

I look at her sitting there in her blue jeans and big old down jacket shrugged off her back. Lark, who's been there and been there and never let me down, who thinks of me and what might give me a smile and even came back when she learned the worst of me. And I think again about never having been loved by an easy person and I wonder if they just never came by, or if it was me never let them in or paid them any mind.

I move a little closer to her, close enough to touch her. My heart's doing things. Pounding and jumping about at the same time and Lark, she's looking up at me, familiar face, sweet, sweet expression while she's waiting on me to tell her it's okay. I put my hand out and even as I do it, I'm fearful she'll jump back or flinch or something, which is stupid. Her hair's soft, thick, heavier than I'd imagined and I run my fingers into it and cup her skull, gentle as I can.

'Nobody ever... I ain't never had a gift like this, Lark,' I tell her.

She lifts her hand and holds onto my wrist, her grip good and steady and she stands. Top of her head just reaches my shoulder and I feel something, really feel something inside and I'm sighing her name and trying to say thank you, for all of it.

'Lark,' I rest my forehead on hers. 'I really...' I don't know how to say it. I don't want to put myself on her, don't want to screw up, but more than anything I don't want to lose her.

She slides her arms inside my blanket. Her hands are warm against my undershirt and my belly melts in on itself. I feel like my legs will give way. To be touched like this, like I hadn't been touched in so long, is almost more than I can stand. I'm mortified by my need. And her touch, my hands on her, hers on me; it is making me breathless.

'What is it?' she asks, real quiet.

'I really like you, Lark.' I whisper it into her hair and right away feel shamed by how lame it is, but she don't laugh at me just murmurs back.

'How *much* do you like me?' And the way she says it makes me laugh in relief.

I pull back and look into her upturned face and her eyes are full of shining humour and something else; a sweet tenderness that pulls me in and hits me a jolt of courage.

'A whole lot.' And I want to tell her so she gets it; that I want to be with her; that she really is the best thing that's ever happened to me and that I sure do hope she still loves me like she said she did.

'I don't think I could do without you, Lark,' I say and I kiss her. Just a question, but she answers me the way I been hoping and the whole world starts to unfold and open.

This morning I got myself up with the sun and left Lark sleeping; she don't need to get up early now school's out for the summer and anyhow, we said our goodbyes last night.

The sunrise is still so low in the sky that as I turn east towards the highway from Main Street, I'm dazzled and need to pull the visor down. A piece of folded paper falls into my lap, but it's not until I stop for a break at a gas station that I read what's on it.

I'll be thinking of you. You're doing such a good thing. Your mother should know she didn't lose two sons, especially when the one left behind is such a good man. And don't shake your head at me like that! I am a better judge of that than you are!

I hope you manage to make a decision about whether to leave John Jnr to rest with his mother or not. Maybe your mother has some ideas about it?

I'll be counting the days till you come home.
Lark.

I read it over, fold it and slide it into my breast pocket and hope that she will always leave notes for me about the place, reminding me that spring comes.

LEAF BY LEAF